Clockwork Spells and Magical Bells

Clockwork Spells and Magical Bells

Edited by
Herika R. Raymer

Clockwork Spells and Magical Bells

Cover Image by Dan Gamber
Cover Design by Allan Gilbreath

Published by
Kerlak Enterprises, Inc.
Kerlak Publishing
Memphis, TN
www.kerlakpublishing.com

ISBN 13: 978-1-937035-10-5
Library of Congress Control Number: 2012934715
First Printing: 2012

Special thanks to everyone at Kerlak Publishing for all of the encouragement and assistance.

This book is printed on acid free paper.

Printed in the United States of America

Copyrights

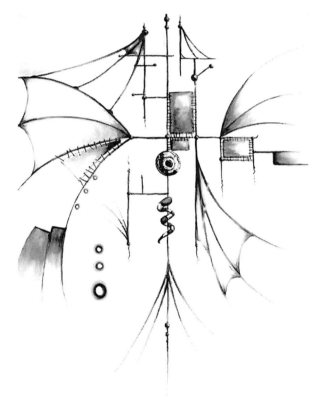

Flying Machines I CAM
by Michael Bielaczyc

Dedication:

To all of the up and coming writers and artists. Never give up on your passions and dreams!

Table of Contents

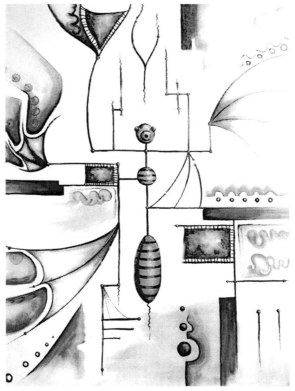

Flying Machines II (NASP)
by Michael Bielaczyc

Foreword

Steampunk.

Strange word, wonderful concept.

Many people ask 'what is steampunk' and while some are ready with an answer still more stumble over their words. I like to think of steampunk as a stylized presentation of the Victorian Age or Western setting, stories where steam engines and clockwork devices are the technology. Recent movies have been set in this background, both new, based on novels or comics, and remakes. Whether or not this adapting to a growing genre will work depends on its presentation. Thankfully, more often than not it has been well received. Yet, as you will hopefully read in the following stories, it can be so much more!

It began with a contest. The contest was one where readers proposed themes to write about for an anthology. Of those ideas, five were selected as the most appealing and presented to a group of authors and artists. The idea behind the experiment? See what the readers wanted, and then encourage the authors and artists to give it to them. The group voted on the one they thought would be the most intriguing: steampunk – with a twist.

Magic versus machine.

The original idea was elves versus dwarves, since most steampunk stories rarely touch this venue. However, the idea was expanded to simply magic versus machine – so long as the machine was steam powered. The authors and artists were challenged, there was no doubt. Yet, the challenge was met by quite a few wonderful tales and we hope that you will enjoy what you read.

Who are these authors and artists? They are small press and self publishing authors as well as amateur and professional artists that live near you. This anthology is to help raise awareness of local talent and encourage you to look, not just in bookstores for big names, but just around the corner for smaller names who tell stories just as well – if not better.

Look at your local book fairs, conventions, even book store events – you will find them there, usually sitting with a few loyal readers. Stop for a moment and chat with them. See if the tales they tell interest you. You never know, you may just have had your own cache of drama, adventure, romance, mystery, or steampunk closer than you thought.

What follows are samples of some talented writers. We certainly hope you enjoy the twist on racing, the agony of hope mislaid, or the triumph of a gamble. We hope the poems make you smile and think. We hope the drawings delight you. Most of all, we hope you look for talent close to you.

Enjoy!

Herika R. Raymer

Ironwork Falcon
Jackie Gamber

Doren Arwood knew machines. He didn't so much build clockwork items as grew them; oiled gears and springs, clips and twisted scraps created themselves into being with the sculptor's touch of Doren's hands. He'd been born for it, or so said his family and friends. And his Dwarven Master, Grel.

It was a rare thing for a human to be apprenticed to another race, let alone a dwarf. Doren was the only one in generations to be honored by such a choice.

Which is why his brother, Efram, was so embarrassing.

Efram was as inept with metals and steam as Doren was gifted. His twin did try. But lately, rather than grasp the tools and getting into Doren's way in the barn stable-turned-workshop, he only watched.

This afternoon, as Doren knelt before his kiln, feeding oak logs into its stone maw and feeling its heat as a stinging rash over his face and chest, he heard Efram's quiet footsteps come to a halt behind him.

"Throw me the splintered one?" he asked, turning aside to open his arms for the catch.

Efram stood in the barn's stone entryway, back-lit by the fierce July sun. His shoulders drooped; his hands were shoved into the pocket of his canvas trousers. One leather suspender held its place over the shoulder of his frayed tunic; the other sagged against his hip.

"The stump right beside your foot," said Doren, still waiting.

His brother finally roused to movement. He bent, and gave a grunt when he lifted the heavy oak stub against his chest. But rather than tossing it, he carried it to Doren and set it into his forearms. "It's not hot enough."

"It's as hot as the stone can handle," Doren said. He shoved the log into the growing blaze, and pushed the kiln's door closed with a pair of snips.

"I know. But it's not enough."

"It's enough." Doren stood, backing one step from the kiln. The barn had already been suffocating when Doren stepped inside to work. Now the place began to take on a heat that choked Doren's throat and sponged breath from his lungs. He removed his tunic and mopped at his face, but it didn't help. The fire only growled toward his skin, trying to roast it.

"You need coal," said Efram.

"I don't have any."

"The blacksmith--"

"Hendridge won't sell me any more until we pay back what's already on our credit." Doren dropped his tunic onto the dusty floor and dragged his charred, cast-off table into a patch of afternoon sun. "Same with the traders, the farmers, and even Mrs. Farran."

That old biddy had been bringing pies and breads to their father in the months since their mother died. Then she began to bring her daughter, Mim, too, who smiled up at Doren with white teeth and bright eyes, offering her own sweet-smelling bread and gooseberry jam. When their father took sick, Mrs. Farran came less often. When their credit became stretched, Mim Farran stopped visiting altogether.

Which was what made Doren so embarrassed. Being a gifted apprentice to a metalworking dwarf didn't bring in the work, when there was no work to be had in their village, the neighboring village, and those beyond. This hunting community had been struck with a tragic and mysterious illness that first dwindled local prey, then their trained hunting birds, and then the people and races who relied on them both, including the Arwood family.

Doren wasn't convinced illness was taking his people as much as starvation and hopelessness, but sometimes it was hard to tell the difference.

"I've begged and borrowed as much as I'm going to," said Doren. "For now, this is where I live. Burning fallen limbs and hammering metals until either the illness takes me too, or I outsmart it."

"With your bird, you mean." Efram kept his distance, glaring at either the kiln or his brother, Doren couldn't quite tell.

"It can work, Eff." Doren hoisted a coiled slab of iron from against the stable wall and thudded it to his table. "Grel told me of the falconer in Brennege that used an eagle to catch a wolf. A wolf!" He looked over his shoulder at his brother and pointed toward a wooden mallet hung by a nail on the near beam. "Can you imagine a bird with the strength of an eagle but the size of a peregrine? Unstoppable. And made of clockwork? Couldn't get sick and die."

"An iron bird can't fly," said Efram. "Let alone hunt."

Doren clenched his jaw. "Mine will. When I'm finished, it will be as light as copper and as strong as a bear."

"Not even you can pound iron into copper with a fire that weak."

Weak? Doren's back felt like scorched leather, and perspiration cascaded from his face and neck and pooled onto the table below. But still, he knew the difference between a wood fire and a coal fire, and even the highest dwarf artisans couldn't pound iron thin enough with even coal. "Then my talent will have to make up for it."

When Efram didn't reply, Doren decided he'd finally won the sporting match of the day. But he looked up to find Efram leaving as silently as he'd entered. "Talent!" he shouted after his brother. "Something you don't know very much about!"

Efram's steps faltered at that. But Doren's self-vindication turned to a barb of shame when Efram cast a dark look over his shoulder. Efram altered his course, and instead of heading into the stone cottage where their father lay dying, he turned toward the path in the surrounding woods.

Doren considered going after him, but determination won out over guilt. He channeled his emotions into his work, as he so often did, and slid his fingers into his suede working gloves, wearing them as weapons against despair.

*****

Days passed in heat and sweat and dehydration delirium. Doren had spent countless hours at his task in the weeks previous, and now he was no nearer to a solution than before. As usual, the inner dials and gears and steam-powered springs, the falcon's innards, chimed and whirred with precision. But its outer casing, with iron-feathered wings, could not lift. He pounded and hammered and trimmed and shaped, but his machine, and his family's salvation, was as grounded as a stone.

And Efram had become scarce. At least he stayed out of Doren's way, leaving him to concentrate, but apart from finding his father in clean bedclothes at night, and with empty soup bowls for breakfast in the morning, Efram left no trace that he resided with them at all.

Leave it to his brother, younger by mere minutes, to dally as a school child in the woods while Doren shouldered the burden of responsibility.

As dawn breathed gray fog, Doren was just piling up the last log of a freshly chopped woodpile. He'd risen early to stoke a hot kiln before the brutal sun added to the misery of his work, but already the air was thick and wet, and heavy as a wool cloak. As determined as he was to be successful, he was sensing looming failure.

And he caught sight of Efram, scuttling from the tool shed behind the house to disappear into the oak and maple arms of their forest.

Doren was suddenly angry. If Efram could make no better use of himself, Doren could at least use his dull brother's strength to stack wood and keep the fire hot. He lunged after him, stomping across the meadow to track him, stop him, and turn him back to home.

But Efram was more agile in the woods than he, and Doren had difficulty following. Burrs caught on his trousers, branches slapped his heat-worn cheeks. Sometimes he would hear sounds in the underbrush, only to spot a rabbit or a squirrel dashing to invisibility. He was just pausing to consider turning back, if he could find his way back, when he went very still, cocked his head, and listened.

Voices. Efram spoke quietly in the distance. The second voice he didn't recognize.

He crept carefully, now more curious than annoyed. He hunkered, allowing low-growing brambles and berry vines to camouflage him. Then, when he was close enough to part leaves and spy through them, he paused.

Efram was easy to spot in a small clearing, where he spoke words Doren didn't know, and waved his hands toward a pile of kindling. At first he smiled at the sight of his oafish brother making awkward, dance-like movements, until he realized Efram didn't look awkward at all. His fingers splayed, and his arms lifted and lowered with a kind of grace. Efram's neck elongated, his wide shoulders straightened. His voice took on a resonance, and, for just a moment, Doren wondered if it was Efram he was watching, after all.

Then the kindling lifted into the air, crashed into each other with the empty thud of a wooden wind chime, and then burst into a fierce explosion of white light and heat. Doren was flattened to the ground, his breath knocked ragged.

"Efram?" he tried to call, stunned. Then he sat up, his wits slowly gathering. "Efram!" he shouted, suddenly on his feet and plunging into the clearing.

Efram turned, white-faced and startled. "Doren?"

Beside Efram, a slender maple tree drew its branches into itself, pulled into the silhouette of a human, and then stepped forward fully as a man. His robes cast outward from his feet like roots, and his skin was the silvery-brown of maple bark.

A forest elf. Doren could feel his upper lip curl in disgust.

The elf opened his arms. "Welcome, brother of Efram."

"Go back to the ground that belched you out," Doren snarled. Then he grasped Efram's elbow and yanked him nearly off his feet.

"Let go, Doren!"

"Back home. Now. Father would soil his deathbed if he knew you were here. With one of them."

"Father does know I'm here!" Efram tightened his arm and broke Doren's grip. "You're not the only one who can apprentice, you know. You have no claim to all the family's talent."

Doren stopped short. "Father knows?" Would Efram lie about something like that?

"He sees them as I do," said Efram. "It is you who refuses to learn from them."

"But they killed our mother! They are killing our father!"

Efram's eyes narrowed. He took a step closer. "Your dwarf master Grel taught you that lie."

Doren looked from Efram to the elf. The elf stood silent and graceful as the trees around them. His pale gaze was calm, steady. "Their magic poisoned the woods," said Doren. "Poisoned our birds. Our people are starving and dying from their atrocity."

"Interesting," said the elf, his voice creaking like a limb in strong wind. "My people believe the same about your master. Digging into Earth's viscera, scavenging without replacing, weakening and sickening her."

"How dare you--"

Efram stepped between them. "I don't begrudge you your training, Doren. Don't begrudge me mine."

"Ha!" Doren didn't have to stand here and defend his beliefs. "Play with the trees all you want, Eff. When you're the next one starving to death, try eating their poison."

Doren plunged through the trees, back toward his barn and his metals, toward the things he could grasp in his hand and feel with fingers. The things of the earth that were solid and real, and that he could see working.

And although he had only a vague idea of the way, he was prepared to walk for hours, rather than to admit he might become lost.

*****

In the night, he heard his father cry out. He scrambled from bed, blind in the darkness, and clumsily made his way along the cool hallway toward his father's room. Efram was already there, lighting a tallow candle and speaking in soothing tones.

"There now," he said. He knelt, taking Father's hand. "I'm here. You can rest."

"My boys," said Father, his voice dry and distant. "My boys."

"Don't give up," said Efram. "Doren works night and day. Soon, his ironwork falcon will fly, and I know you'll want to see it when it does."

"Yes." Father smiled faintly, his eyes still closed. "He is a gift."

"Yes," said Efram. He turned his face toward Doren, his dark eyes rimmed with moisture. "He is."

Tears threatened Doren, too. The fatigue and disappointment of the past weeks rushed in, all at once, to overwhelm him. He braced against the wooden door frame.

"And so are you," said Father, reaching for Efram's hand.

Doren pushed away from the door frame, managing to reach Efram before he, too, collapsed to his knees. "And so are you, Eff," he echoed.

"My boys," said Father.

*****

Doren awoke with a stiff neck and swollen eyes. He lifted his head, orienting. He'd fallen asleep on his knees, beside his father's bed, still clasping his father's hand. For a moment, he was startled at the peaceful look on his father's face, but realized his hand was warm. Father was breathing.

He rose slowly, working out kinks in his back and legs. Then he began to walk toward the galley kitchen, but paused at the sounds coming from the barn. Efram was in his workshop.

He crossed the dawn-weary meadow toward the barn, and leaned into the entryway. "Taking up my tools?" he asked.

Efram faintly startled, and spun, eying his brother sheepishly. "Not your tools. Your kiln."

"My kiln?"

"I've been practicing a spell no elf mage has mastered," he said. "It creates a white-hot flame to soften metal, without burning skin."

Doren straightened. "You can do that?"

"I'm not very good at it yet, but I will be."

Doren canted his head. "Softening metal without wood. Without coal."

Efram lifted his shoulders. "A little wood. But no coal."

"I don't want any magic in my falcon."

"No," said Efram, shaking his head. "That's all you. I only want to give you a fire."

Doren smiled. "All right, then, little brother. Let's see what you've got."

Efram smiled too, his eyes bright. "Yeah?"

"Yeah." He stuck out his hand, and Efram clasped and pumped it eagerly.

Efram started to circle the kiln, speaking quietly. And Doren turned to pull his charred, cast-off table closer, to lay out his tools.

Behind them, their father stood weakly in the door frame, watching them. Smiling.

"My boys," he said.

Discombobulation
Robert J. Krog

One of the peculiarities of working in a clock shop is that one becomes accustomed to the ticks, the tocks, the chimes, and the bells to the point that one hardly notices them. They become like one's heartbeat. One thinks of incessant noise as one thinks of silence, and one finds silence somehow unnatural. If one does not become accustomed to the noise, one must quit the work or go insane.

Feono the Dwarf became accustomed and spent his days tinkering with clocks and adding to Master Clockmaker Harmon's inventory some ingenious models that only the mind of a dwarf could conceive. With his shop in good hands, Harmon, a human, took up the making of safes on which he collaborated with the elf wizard, Sseleman, and which they then sold to the railroads. For ten years, due to Harmon's engineering and Sseleman's spellcraft, no bandits profited from a payroll heist when a Harmon-Sseleman safe protected the cash. Throughout the badlands, they were roundly cussed for a decade.

Even bandits have their days, and it came to pass that a Harmon-Sseleman safe was breached in the eleventh year of their run, and a great deal of money was stolen. It was Sseleman's apprentice, Talmin, who brought the news to Feono, on a blustery, spring day. He sauntered in, dry of course - the first spell every apprentice used to show off was the dry-walking spell - and tossed the morning paper down atop Feono's work bench.

"Good morning, my large-nosed, black-bearded friend," said the Elf.

Moving the paper aside and barely glancing up, Feono responded, "Good morning my pointy-eared, pointy-nosed friend."

Looking at the headline, Feono read,

"NOTHING LASTS FOREVER – HARMON SAFE CRACKED, SSELEMAN ENCHANTMENT DISPELLED."

Harmon's daughter, Helen, got up from her work bench and read over Feono's shoulder. "Oh, that's horrible. Daddy could be ruined."

Feono shook his head as he perused the article. "It's part of the business and was bound to happen some time or other. He'll just have to change the design. I'm sure he won't be happy with the news, though."

"Master Sseleman's reputation is at stake now, too," said Talmin, "but mainly from a human perspective. We elves take a longer view. It'll be an interesting challenge. I can't imagine how they overcame the protective spells. The wizard working with the robbers has to be a master in his own right."

"He's a murderer, too," said Feono, "Three of the payroll guards were killed and one of them by magic."

Talmin shook his head at that.

"I'd better tell father," said Helen, picking up the paper and heading off into the back of the shop.

"I'll go with you," said Feono, sliding off his workbench and jogging after her.

"I'll guess I'll just sit here with all these clocks," said Talmin.

"Someone has to keep an eye out for shoplifters," said Feono.

* * *

Harmon was busy counting out the right number of rivets for the latest refinement of his masterful design. Back bent from age and work, he leaned over his workbench from atop a three-legged stool.

"Daddy, you aren't going to believe this," said Helen, thrusting the paper at him.

"I didn't finish the article," said Feono from behind her, "but it was leading up to how they did it. If the safe wasn't carried off, the railroad will probably want you to examine it."

"Yes, yes," murmured Harmon distractedly, taking the paper and adjusting his eyeglasses.

They stood there, Feono patient, Helen huffing, while Harmon took his time reading the article.

"Well?" demanded the girl.

"Well, what?" asked Harmon after a moment.

"Isn't it dreadful?"

"Yes. Men were killed in the robbery. That is dreadful."

"Well, right," said Helen, suddenly biting her lip.

"I'll want to contribute some money to the widows, if there are any," said Harmon.

"Right," said Helen.

Harmon kept reading. After another minute or two, Helen asked, "Daddy, will the railroad still want you to make safes for them?"

He peered at her over the edge of the paper, wisps of white hair dangling in front of his eyes, "I don't know, but I shall certainly examine the broken safe and offer an improvement. I think Sseleman will want to do the same from his end."

Unsure of what to say to his unruffled composure, she made an excuse and left.

"If you need assistance collecting the safe and looking it over," offered Feono.

"I'm sure I will, my boy, I'm sure I will," said Harmon, still reading.

Amused at being called a boy by a human whose age was a third of his own, Feono returned to his workbench in the storefront.

* * *

They collected the safe from the railroad a day later. The thing was completely, and neatly, disassembled, every screw, every rivet having been removed.

"Now why would they do that?" asked Feono as he and Talmin loaded the safe into the trunk of Harmon's steam car.

Sseleman, standing reservedly beside Harmon said, "I think the wizard was showing off. It was surely done by magic."

"Humph," grunted Feono, hefting one wall of the safe into the trunk.

"You have to admit that it's pretty showy," said Talmin.

"Admire him if you like," said Feono, "but I don't admire a murderer, however clever he may be."

"You're such a curmudgeon," said Talmin.

* * *

Three days later, news of another successful heist against a Harmon-Sseleman safe was in the morning papers. Feono had the paper in front of him already when Talmin entered the shop.

"Already read it," he told the elf, "so you're not bringing news."

Talmin smirked his best elf-smirk at that, "I have news that isn't in the paper."

"Really?"

"Really. Master Sseleman figured out the spell they used, and will develop an enchantment to block it by tonight, probably. He's very good, you know."

"Good news, I should say."

"I'd like to show you the spell," declared the elf.

17

"The one that disassembled the safe?"

"Yes."

"Surely not in here."

"Don't worry about it. I can clean up after."

Feono raised an eyebrow, but gestured for him to proceed.

"The spell," said Talmin, "has been titled 'discombobulation.' That's my word for it."

"Is that a real word?"

"It is," said Talmin. He recited the spell while pointing at a desktop clock. Feono watched, and, at the end of the recitation, the clock came apart. Every tiny screw came out. Each part of the little machine separated neatly from each other part. Helen, who had just entered the room, walked up amazed and looked back and forth from Talmin to the disassembled clock.

"That's how the robber-wizard did it?" she asked.

"So Master Sseleman seems to think," said Feono, examining the results.

"That's precisely how he did it," Talmin assured them.

Feono saw that there wasn't one piece connected to another.

"It seems unnecessarily complete," he said to the elf, "It would have sufficed to discombobulate the door."

"It's rather flamboyant," admitted Talmin.

"Discombobulate?" asked Helen, "Is that a word?"

"So our pointy-eared friend says," said the dwarf.

She raised a blond eyebrow and shook her head. "I've never heard that word," she said.

"I'm one hundred and ninety years old," said Talmin, "consider the possibility that I've heard some words you haven't."

"Feono has a hundred years on you, and he's never heard it, have you, Feono?" she asked.

He looked up from the remains of the clock, "This is the first time, but that doesn't prove anything."

"I don't think it's a word," she said.

Talmin ignored that and stepped up beside Feono. "It worked perfectly the first time," he crowed.

Feono rewarded him with a skeptical expression, "You've never worked a spell perfectly the first time. No one does, or so you've said before."

"First time for everything," said the elf, and he changed subject. "Have you told Master Harmon about the second heist?"

Feono nodded, "He's designing a new safe. Master Sseleman is working on new spells to protect it from magic?"

"That he is."

Feono looked at the mess and then looked meaningfully at Talmin. Talmin smiled back, very pleased.

"You took it apart…" prompted the dwarf.

"What? I have to put it back together?"

Helen interjected, "It's only fair. It's some work assembling a clock like that."

It wasn't much work, but Feono let the statement stand. He was faster than Helen.

"Very well," said Talmin, and he grinned, "It's two minutes work for me. I can reverse the spell."

"Combobulate?" asked Helen.

"Exactly." He recited the magic words, adding gestures not included before. The pieces of the clock reassembled themselves as they watched. Feono kept a close eye, and doubted that it was put together quite right. When the spell was done, he went over to wind the clock and knew as soon as he turned the knob that a spring wasn't engaged. He shook his head at the elf.

"It's never as easy to put something together as it is to take it apart," he said.

"Oh, come on. You're saying it's not right?" asked Talmin.

"I'm saying," said Feono.

Talmin shrugged, "I've done most of the work for you."

"About as much as I could expect. Thanks for demonstrating the spell."

Talmin bowed elegantly and turning to Helen said, "For my reward, I would like a cup of wine and some of that sweet bread you make."

She smacked at him but led him away to the kitchen to find what he sought.

Feono took the clock to the back workroom to put it together correctly. He found Harmon busy at his drafting table and Sseleman there beside him.

Man and elf were in deep conversation, so Feono went to the tool cabinet without saying a word.

"I don't understand it," said the wizard, "It would take either an arch-mage, or nearly an arch-mage, or someone with an already intimate knowledge of them, to undo my spells. What arch-mage would need to stoop to train robbery to make a living when he could make a far easier and just as lucrative living without committing crimes?"

"Was there something more than cash in the safe?" asked Harmon.

"I've spoken with the railroad's security chief, and he assured me that the safe only contained payroll cash."

"It is a conundrum," said Harmon.

Feono found the tool he needed and was about to go, when Harmon asked, "Tell me again how the disassemble spell works."

"Talmin wants me to call it 'discombobulate,' which is not the right word," said Sseleman, smiling at his apprentice's whimsy, "And I don't know what it's inventor calls it, though I'd like to ask him if he ever gets caught."

"Is 'discombobulation' a real word?" asked Harmon, frowning.

Feono suppressed a chuckle.

"The spell works by taking apart things that are joined mechanically. The wizard orders all the nuts, bolts, screws, springs, nails, rivets, what have you, to retract and come apart, and they do."

"He has to name them?" asked Harmon.

"Yes."

"Then if I put in some unusual fasteners, we might confound the wizard and slow him down?"

Sseleman nodded, "Yes, that would work." An idea occurred to him, suddenly, and he exclaimed, "Or you could use welds. That's a more than mechanical bond."

Harmon shook his head tolerantly, "A safe that's welded shut won't be useful."

Abashed, the wizard nodded his agreement, "Sorry. Silly idea."

"I could weld most of the safe together, but the door would still have to be dead bolted and worked by combination."

Sseleman nodded, "Using unusual fasteners would keep the body of the safe together, but what about the door? Are there any alternatives to the usual tumblers and such?"

"I can think of something, I'm sure, and Feono might have some ideas. Dwarves have fasteners in their machines that most humans and elves wouldn't know about."

Sseleman nodded, considered and said, "But all we're really doing is slowing him down."

Harmon said, "If he gets past your protective spells, all I can do is make the safe as tough as possible to discombobulate and damage. He won't want to do enough damage to the safe that he destroys the payroll."

"You could make two safes of two different designs," said Feono, "one inside the other. That would slow him down more. I'll sketch some dwarfish fasteners for you, too."

They looked up, only just realizing that he was there. After a moment, Feono added, "That's working on the assumption that the discombobulate spell can only function on one discrete machine at a time?"

Sseleman nodded slowly, "It does. That's a good idea."

"What about adding parts in motion?" asked the dwarf, approaching the drafting table. "If someone was winding the thing up periodically so that the things were moving like fast clockwork on the inside, would that confound the wizard's attempts further?"

Sseleman considered that, "It would," he said, "Even so, parts not in motion would be affected."

"We could design it so that it would jam shut in such a contingency," suggested Harmon.

Feono took a seat on a stool, pleased to be in on the project.

* * *

Harmon and Sseleman put together a pair of ingenious, new safes with Feono's help and had them assembled and sold to the railroads in record time, though not fast enough to prevent another robbery. They awaited the papers eagerly after that.

* * *

Another morning came that Talmin entered the shop bearing the morning paper. "It was a bloody affair," said the elf, "they killed twenty armed guards, lost three of their own, and made off with a payroll again."

"Damn," said Feono. "I guess we slowed them down, though."

"Enough that they had to fight their way out," said Talmin. He added, "In addition to the new safes, the railroads are beefing up their security forces."

Helen had her hand to her mouth in horror, but said, "Maybe the robbers won't try again, now that it's so dangerous."

"They've only netted… they can't have made off with more than ten or twenty thousand a piece. They'll want more before they quit."

Feono said grimly, "They could just as likely feel angry and that they have a score to settle. They may try harder. Since they beat the safe designs, they'll be able to do it faster the next time." He bristled with annoyance.

"Don't take it so hard," said Talmin, "They beat our spells too. When I helped Master Sseleman enchant the safes, I saw how clever the work was. You couldn't have done more."

Feono couldn't help but feel that there was something more he could have done, only he didn't know what.

There was no banter that day.

* * *

On the next day, a letter came from one of the railroad companies stating that Harmon-Sseleman were now merely in the running to produce the best safes. The company was looking at other contractors. They wanted a solution to their problem. Talmin said Master Sseleman had received a copy, too. Soon, Sseleman and Harmon were ensconced in Harmon's workroom, redesigning.

Feono, Talmin, and Helen sat in the storefront killing time. Helen dealt with customers while the other two played cards.

"I wish they'd let me in on the designing," said Talmin.

Feono said, "I thought Master Sseleman had your help designing spells."

Talmin shook his head, "I designed a spell not too long ago, but it was for myself. Master Sseleman never thinks he needs my help, whatever ideas I have. It's a hapless life being his apprentice. I should've sought a human master, like you."

Feono shook his head, "I didn't seek a human master. I arrived and found that the dwarves I was supposed to meet here for a business venture never made it. I took a job where I was sure my skills would be useful and remunerated. I started to like Master Harmon, before long, and realized I could learn from him, so I stayed. When he dies, if I don't get the business, I'll pay my respects and move on."

"Surely, he'll leave you the business," said Talmin.

"I suspect that depends on Helen's choice of a husband, whether or not the fellow is well-to-do. He has to think of her first. I'll have other prospects, and he knows it."

Talmin harrumphed in a very unelfish manner, and Feono chuckled.

"I wish I knew what they were doing in there," said Talmin again.

"Eh, I'll help Master Harmon put it together. If you're that interested, I'll fill you in, but it's probably more technical than you'd care to hear."

"I just want us to succeed," said Talmin.

"We'll succeed," Feono assured him, "besides, it's the magic that's more important. You'll be in on all that when you help Master Sseleman enchant the safes, won't you?"

"Yeah, I'll be there for that part."

"Then why worry?"

"Yeah," muttered the elf, "why worry? It's only our livelihoods at stake."

"You've lived among humans too long. Elves take the long view, remember?"

Talmin kept the worried expression.

* * *

When Sseleman and Talmin had gone home, Harmon came in and invited Feono out for drink with him.

"Sseleman suspects someone is spying on us," he whispered to the dwarf, once they were seated at a local bar.

"Just us or them too?" asked Feono, also whispering.

"Both, he thinks. He's spelled me and you against eavesdropping and such, but he's worried someone's spying with magic. He wants you to add something to the defense of the safes without telling me what it is. You can install it on the train yourself."

"You mean a booby trap?" asked Feono.

Harmon nodded, "A separate machine, too, so there will actually be at least three to disassemble before the robbers get to the money. Sseleman's designing a magical trap we won't know about."

"I'm at his service, of course," said the Dwarf, "and yours."

"Good," said Harmon.

* * *

It wasn't hard for Feono to address the problem. He'd been thinking about something on those lines already. His booby trap was completed in two days. He did it on his own time, using parts from the shop so anyone spying on him would probably think he was working on a clock. He did have to get a few items from a gun maker, but he did that at times when Harmon and Sseleman were at work together, so anyone watching or listening by whatever means, would likely be concentrating on them.

A week after he finished his booby trap, they were installing the latest double safe on the train most likely to be robbed. Feono kept the trap hidden until the safes were installed, then after Harmon was finished, he stayed a moment to "gather up the equipment" and slipped the trap into the space between the two safes. It fit snugly, and, if his care had been adequate, no one but he knew. It would only be a danger to someone using the "discombobulate" spell on the first safe. Satisfied, he gathered up the equipment and went to join Harmon in the car. Harmon was reminding the security chief to wind the safe up every half hour to keep the clockwork inside moving to confuse the robber-wizard's efforts. Feono tossed his equipment case in the trunk and climbed into the passenger seat. Harmon gave him a questioning look. He nodded. They drove away.

* * *

That evening, Talmin arrived with a bottle of wine to toast their efforts.

"So fill me in on what it was I helped enchant yesterday afternoon, big-nose," he said to Feono, "Will it foil the robber-wizard or not?"

"It'll slow him down at least, pointy-ears," said Feono, wishing he could tell somebody about his booby trap but remembering that magical eyes and ears might be listening in. The booby trap might do more than slow down the wizard thief, but, if it worked, he'd take credit for it then.

"Well, what's special about this latest design?" asked Talmin, pouring into the wine glasses that Helen brought from the kitchen.

"They're not telling," said Helen, "or hadn't you noticed?"

"Seriously?" asked Talmin, amazed, "It's only us."

"We're worn out, and it's so much effort to describe," said Feono. He groped for a way to explain without giving anything away to prying eyes or ears.

"Oh, come on," said the elf, "What new dwarfish technology have you incorporated into the design?"

"Oh, the same deal as before," said Feono, a little annoyed at Talmin's persistence and his own need for secrecy, "Moving parts, rivets where there were bolts and vice versa, things like that. One fastener or joiner type substituted for another." He didn't mention that they had welded shut the loops for the springs and attached them to closed rings instead of open hooks. That was a new ingredient that should baffle a discombobulate spell, they hoped.

"Whatever you say," said Talmin, deflating, "I hope it works this time."

"I think it'll work," said Feono, raising his glass, "Here's to our enemies losing blood, and if not that, at least may they be confounded."

"Here, here," said Helen.

"Here, here," muttered Talmin.

They all drank, refilled, and drank some more. Helen told a joke.

"Two peanuts walk into a bar," she said, "but only one walks out, why?"

"I don't know," answered Feono, "why?"

"Because," she giggled, "the other one was a salted. Get it? It was a salted."

Feono frowned then got it. He laughed. Talmin shook his head in disgust.

"We could have no income in a few days if another heist succeeds, and you're making puns."

"I can't help it," said Helen, "Your wine's gone straight to my head." She giggled more.

"I'll cry about that if it happens," said Feono, "Perk up, pointy-ears, we aren't done yet."

Talmin drained his glass and poured another.

"Do you plan on staying the night, or must I carry you home?" asked Feono, watching the elf drain the third glass.

"I'll be fine," said Talmin, crossly, "I never met a dwarf who could out drink me."

"I wouldn't dream of trying," said Feono, "but you're in a bad mood. If the wine isn't lightening it, maybe you should ease up."

"I don't take drinking advice from dwarves," said Talmin, but he only took a swallow from his cup. "That damnable robber-wizard and his discombobulate spell have caused me no end of headaches."

"Isn't his dispelling ability just as problematical?" asked Feono.

"Oh, those are fairly standard. It just takes a lot of power or a good knowledge of exactly what spells were used to enchant the safes. The discombobulate spell, now that's the bit of genius. Overkill, it's true, but ingenious, nevertheless. I congratulate him on it, but I find it very inconvenient.

"Look at me, look at me, I'm the robber-wizard," he said, slurring his words slightly. He drained the fourth glass and started reciting the spell. He pointed at a wall clock, and it disassembled, clattering on the floor. A spring shot across the room, landing in Helen's lap. She giggled and refilled her wine glass. Feono sighed, but decided not to protest.

"Robber-wizard, robber-wizard," said Talmin, "what a genius, what a pain in the butt." He recited the spell again, pointing at a coo-coo clock a few feet away.

"Wait," warned Feono, but the clock, more tightly wound than the wall clock, and with faster moving parts, all but exploded, showering the three of them with clockwork pieces. A flying gear shattered Feono's glass, spilling wine on his lap.

"Nice," he said, picking shards from his lap and beard.

"Oops," said Talmin, giggling alongside Helen.

"Talmin, Talmin," said Feono, "be careful what you discombobulate. Some machines are dangerous when they come apart. Imagine doing that to a steam engine for a train or factory. You could kill somebody. The fine line between mischief and crime is crossed when someone gets hurt. You're the only friend I have who's even close to my age. I'd rather you didn't get crushed or burned to death."

As he said it, he realized that, in maturity, Sseleman, far older, and Harmon, far younger, where much more his peers. Talmin was about the same level in maturity as a human boy not yet twenty. Talmin tried to cover his mirth but succeeded only in burping, which set Helen to laughing.

A little later, Feono helped Helen into her bed and settled Talmin into his, though the elf's feet hung over. Feono slept on a cot in Harmon's workroom. When he woke in the morning, Talmin was gone. Helen was hung over and no good that day.

The morning paper brought no bad news, so Feono and Harmon spent the day working in the shop. Evening came and Sseleman stopped by. He came in by the back door, as usual, and found Feono hard at work reassembling the coo-coo clock.

"Wasn't that on the wall yesterday?" asked the wizard.

"It was, but your errant apprentice was demonstrating the magic of our esteemed enemy."

Sseleman raised an eyebrow, "I wasn't aware he'd mastered that spell."

"He's a very talented fellow, friend Talmin is," said Feono, never missing an opportunity to put in good word for his friend. He kept his eyes on his work, though.

"Well, I've tried hard to train him up. Is he here?"

Feono frowned. It wasn't like Talmin to be out of his master's range of call. "He was into the drink a bit. He brought a bottle over and wasn't too steady on his feet. I put him in my bed for the night. Slept on a cot in the workroom myself. He was gone this morning, though. I thought he'd reported back to you." He glanced up at the wizard.

Sseleman ran a hand through his hair. "Foolishness," he muttered, "The boy was talking about us helping protect the payrolls more directly, but I told him that's not our business. I hope he hasn't taken it upon himself."

Feono put his tools aside and stood. "Perhaps we should go find him."

"Stay at your work. I'll locate the boy." Sseleman turned to go. "Into the corn liquor was he?" he asked when he noted the second clock in pieces.

"No," said Feono, sitting again, "it was wine."

"Hmm. He must have been drinking before he arrived. He can down three bottles of that wine of his before he wobbles. Well, I'll find him and set him straight."

He went to the door and paused there. "Feono," he said.

"Yes, Master Sseleman?"

"That special task, the particular clock I asked Harmon about. Is it ready?"

Feono nodded.

The wizard nodded back. "Thank you for that." He walked out and Feono resumed his work, troubled. It wasn't like Talmin to disappear. The young fool couldn't have gone off to defend trains from bandits, he told himself, but he worried anyway.

* * *

The next morning came and Talmin didn't arrive with a paper in hand, so Feono went out and bought one. The headline was this: ROBBER-WIZARD KILLED IN ATTEMPTED HEIST: REIGN OF TERROR OVER: HARMON-SSELEMAN SAFES ON TOP AGAIN! Thrilled, Feono sprinted back to the shop and burst in shouting for Helen and Harmon. They dashed up, and he read the headline aloud. They whooped and hollered while Feono tried to read the article over their noise. He had to read about the dead wizard twice before it sunk in.

"A young elf, possibly in business in the city, was found to be the robber-wizard. He was killed by an explosion, the source of which is unclear, either from the attempt to open the safe by magic or explosives or from a booby-trap."

Helena and Harmon both sank onto a workbench.

"There aren't but what, three young elves in the city?" asked Harmon, "but it couldn't be him, could it?"

"He's the only one with any significant magical talent," said Feono, with horror in his voice and eyes. He too found a seat.

"But the discombobulate spell doesn't make things blow up, I mean, not a safe, not like that. Not enough to kill anyone," protested Helen.

"It's my doing," said Feono, staring at the floor.

"What do you mean?" she asked.

"They wanted a solution, and your father and Master Sseleman asked me to make a booby trap but not to tell anyone, because they suspected someone was spying on us. I made a bomb that I could slide between the walls of the two safes, a bomb that would be primed by being wedged in and detonated if the tension was released by one of the safes being discombobulated."

"Oh, my God," said Helen, tears starting into her eyes finally.

"Oh the poor boy, the poor, foolish boy," said Harmon, wiping a tear from his face.

Feono wanted to weep too, but dwarves don't weep easily and certainly not for dead enemies, so he forced them back by will alone and stood. "Pity us instead of him. Pity Sseleman rather than a murdering traitor. Recall, he killed with magic in at least one robbery. Don't pity Talmin." He put a hand on each of their shoulders, squeezed, and went back to his work.

Helen wept a little anyway, then Harmon took her out. The clocks ticked away. The hour came, and the clocks chimed. The little birds popped out and coo-cooed. Talmin would not be coming in that morning to break up the monotony of the day, nor any day thereafter. In a few years, Feono would stop looking for him and miss him no more. In hundred years or so, he probably wouldn't think of him unless reminded. In the meantime, the incessant noise of the shop would drown out the silence left behind by Talmin's departure, so long as Feono remembered to listen to it. In a clock shop, though, one becomes accustomed to the noise. It is like silence, and more often than not, he didn't even notice it, and he longed for some cheerful, familiar face to come in and break up the monotony of the day.

Moved To Action
Angelia Sparrow

"Good people, the Diversatile Mechanical Servant is the modern solution to the servant problem. Capable of executing twenty different commands, it serves most household needs. Mechanical servants eliminate most of the common problems associated with servants, such as sloth, theft, idleness, abandoning their post and abolitionists."

An ugly murmur went through the crowd at the mention of the thieves headed by petticoats and Quakers. Simon Green looked out over them and gauged his next words as a pretty blond woman shook off her chaperone's hold on her arm and made her way to the front, near the stage. She gave him a flirtatious look and then stared up at the shiny machine.

Simon had to admit the Diversatile was shiny. He extolled its virtues for another two minutes and then slid a thin brass plate, with holes in a very specific pattern, into the Command Slot on the side of the thing's head.

"I have given the machine a task," he informed the crowd as the servant walked to a pile of laundry that had been set out nearby. It folded a man's shirt, neatly as if it had been pressed. "The Diversatile can fold clothing, wash clothing, sweep a floor, polish shoes or silver, dust, make beds and many more tasks. Simply insert the proper plate into the Command slot and the Diversatile is ready to obey. Oil it once a week, wind it once a day, and it will give you years of unstinting service. That is all the care he requires, for should he ever fail, return him to our facility for repairs or replacement at no charge. More task plates are in the works. Imagine the luxury of having but a single servant, which requires no food, no rest and no accommodation."

"It seems to me, Sir, that a man could buy one of those and never need a wife. Is it your intent to render my sex obsolete?"

The blond woman's chaperone covered her face in shame at her charge's boldness. Simon just laughed. He'd often heard the same sentiment, from both worried ladies and confirmed bachelors.

"Dear lady, as long as ladies are as lovely and fast-thinking as yourself, they will never be obsolete." Flattery got him almost everywhere.

She harrumphed and her chaperone caught up with her, guiding her away from the stage so he could finish. He did so, and after the presentation, hopped off the stage to find the pretty lady.

"Dear miss, may I offer you and your lovely sister a tour of the factory where the Diversatile is made? Perhaps you could offer suggestions as to the next task it should be made capable of."

She offered a calling card with one hand. "You may call upon me tomorrow in the afternoon, sir." She trailed after her chaperone and vanished into the afternoon throng at the dime museum.

Simon went through his pitch for the next group of spectators, his mind haunted by blonde curls and flirty blue eyes belonging to Miss Malvina Kesler.

The call went well, and on the following Thursday, Miss Malvina and her maiden aunt, Calisty, came for a tour of the factory. Simon had taken all precautions he could and led them through the showroom.

"This is the prototype for the next generation of Diversatile Mechanical Servant. It's not ready for public demonstration, yet."

The ladies watched the servant set out a tea tray, put cups, a teapot, creamer and sugar bowl on it. It picked up the tray and walked across the room to set it on a low table. A foot from the tabletop it dropped the tray, and all the breakables shattered.

Simon shook his head. "Alas, it happens every time. There is a problem with the depth perception."

He guided them on to the painting room, where pretty Irish and German girls in white dresses put the delicate facial features onto the servants. They watched the whole process, from blank face to fully painted. He steered them onward into the polishing room, where fair-skinned Negro girls used brass polish and cloths to make sure every Diversatile shone before it came to the sales floor.

"I still say you will destroy the livelihood of many servants and end many marriages. They may be useful for old widowers who have no wives or daughters. But I think the breakage will preclude them becoming popular."

"Can we see them being assembled, Mr. Green?" Calisty asked.

"I'm sorry, ladies, that is a company secret." He led them on toward a reception room and a neatly dressed mulatto girl served tea without dropping anything.

Malvina and her aunt sipped the tea as was proper. Simon had a second cup to steady his nerves in the wake of the glances Malvina was shooting at him. When he saw the pixie sitting in the chandelier it was much too late to do anything but topple backwards, unconscious.

* * *

Malvina awoke, not in the nice reception room on the shiny red horsehair sofa, but trussed up like a turkey and lying on the floor. She saw feet moving around her, and hooves as well. Hooves? She squirmed to get more comfortable and see. Aunt Calisty and that nice Mr. Green were nowhere to be seen.

"She awake." The soft Gullah slur on the words and the large black hand that turned her head frightened her.

More hooves, about the size of a colt or a small pony, trotted over. The legs were glossy chestnut, with black marking.

"Good afternoon, Miss. I must apologize for the straits in which you find yourself, but your tour coincided with our general revolt and now you and your chaperone are valuable hostages."

Malvina looked up, searching for the source of the voice. She saw the handsome man talking to her and decided he must be riding the pony, for surely there were no such things as centaurs in the real world. They were creatures from mythology lessons.

The large black hands helped her sit up and she stared some more. Half a dozen centaurs, twenty or so Negro men and a whole raft of pixies filled the room.

"Dear God, where am I?" she asked as she felt her tenuous hold on consciousness waver. Delicate brown fingers held smelling salts under her nose.

"Take you all for a pack of fools, startling her so." One of the polishing girls held her up. "I'm Cassandra, Miss. This bunch, they aren't bad at heart, but they been talking too much, reading too much. Tashunka worse than the others." She gestured at a pinto centaur with high native cheekbones and long black hair that flowed into his black mane.

"What's going on? What happened?" Malvina felt silly for asking, but women of her stature simply didn't associate with people like the ones she found herself around.

"We're having an action," Tashunka said, his words accented. "Our working conditions are intolerable and we cannot endure them longer. So

41

we have taken action. You are our insurance that Mr. Green will negotiate rather than simply gas us all and buy new workers."

"Insurance? Gas?" She shook her head. Surely the nice Mr. Green, so smart and charming, wouldn't harm anyone. "I'm a hostage?"

"We prefer to think of you as a guest and negotiator for our situation," Tashunka clopped closer, his hooves very black. As he drew near, Malvina could see sores on his withers and scarring on his back and flanks.

She got to her feet, bracing against the pounding in her head. She didn't faint often and she recovered quickly, if she wasn't too tightly laced. Tashunka was taller than she was, his withers about four and a half feet high and his human shoulders easily six feet off the ground.

"Where is my aunt? It is highly inappropriate for me to be in this room without a chaperone." She looked around. All the polishing girls had taken off their uniforms and were standing around in their shimmys. The human men wore only drawers and the centaurs wore nothing. Scandalous behavior was only to be expected of this class, but the amount of exposed flesh left her quite giddy.

"Your aunt and the young Mr. Green are being held elsewhere in the mines. Flit." Tashunka beckoned and a pixie floated down to him. "Take a message to where the other hostages are, let them know that young miss has woken and is in good spirits."

Flit bounced in mid-air and sped off. Malvina tracked the little ball of light until it vanished around the corner. Tashunka and the other centaurs got comfortable, and the humans found seats on the floor until Malvina was the only one left standing. Cassandra offered her a low stool, but she decided to stay upright. She didn't like the way some of the men eyed her.

"Pretty white girl don't know what's what. She thinkin' everything below as easy and pretty as above," one of the men said, his tone nasty.

"Needs educating," Cassandra said. "Maybe polishing until she can't move her arms?"

"Maybe pulling an ore cart out of the mines. They used to use Irish girls for that until they got permission to take the native and centaur tribes for slaves," Tashunka suggested.

A tall human man, with features similar to Tashunka's, but skin a little darker, just glowered. "Maybe she's delicate enough to do pixie work. We hang her in a cage and let her die from poisonous gas to warn us."

"Don't be ridiculous!" Malvina snapped. "Those sort of things are just horror stories out of a Knights of Labor pamphlet. Or an abolitionist tract. Pure nonsense." She crossed her arms and looked up and away.

This, however, made her look at the pixies. The little beings perched on a ledge, most of them slumping, some with torn wings, some barely glowing. Several of them coughed. All of them were stained black with coal dust. One coughed and coughed, unable to stop, until it crumpled into a silent, darkened heap.

She heard and felt a centaur's approach. It was not Tashunka, but a buckskin, his hair shaved on the sides of his head until the top stood up like his mane. His coppery skin blended into the tan of the horse-hide, both of them lighter than Tashunka.

"Is this nonsense, girl?" His large hand turned her to look at him.

The whip-welts crossed his torso in pale streaks. Large sores ran in a line down from his shoulders to meet a similar line at his human waist and a y-shaped line going between his forelegs. A bald patch in his mane just in front of his withers matched a very large calloused area.

"What?" she asked. "What did this?" Her fingers brushed his skin very lightly, staying away from the sores. The contact sent an odd tingling sensation through her. She had touched others' hands, and this was no different. No different at all, despite him being a centaur and an Indian.

"Years of ore carts drawn out of the mine. Tin and copper and brass don't bubble to the surface of the earth on their own."

Cassandra came and sat beside her, in an overly familiar way. "Chogan is in bad shape. The owners try to take care of their property. It's getting harder and more expensive to replace us."

A pixie darted in and talked to Tashunka. He gave a sharp whistle. "The owners have plotted our location. Take the food and water. We're relocating to the secondary command post." As Cassandra and the centaurs gathered supplies, Tashunka called the black men in to a huddle and they held a hasty conference. Four black men, each carrying a heavy looking pick, left.

Malvina swallowed hard. She suspected they were being sent to act as a rear-guard. Cassandra and two of the other polishing girls handed her bundles. She staggered under the weight of the parcels, noticing the other handled them with relative ease, and then juggled them until she saw how they were carrying their loads. After slinging them across her back, she realized that she had her own bodyguards in the strong-armed women-- bodyguards or jailers, she wasn't sure which.

Tashunka led the way deeper into the mines, the pixies sitting on the brim of his helmet illuminating the path. Two of them settled in Malvina's hair. They weighed no more than a moth, but they jingled most annoyingly. It was worse than the belled Christmas bonnet two years before.

The air grew colder and smelled bad. Strange odors, not of cooking or people, drifted past Malvina until she suspected they were walking to Hell itself. Nobody else seemed to notice. Down several side tunnels, she saw miners, all Negro or native, mostly human, sitting quietly with pixies on their helmets. No work was being done for the factory.

Deep in the mines, they finally came to a large cavern. Malvina caught her breath at the sight of dozens of children in ragged clothes down here, watched over by the girls she had seen in the painting room. The children were of all colors, the dark ones ashy from lack of sun, the pale ones peaked from the same. Their spindly limbs and lank hair made her want to cry. She had seen beggar children often enough, but so many in one place clutched at her heart. The Irish and German girls moved through the crowd, handing out bread and bowls of thin soup. She watched a little girl reach up and realized with a shock she only had three fingers above the bandage on her hand.

Her captors hurried her through here, taking her still deeper. "Mr. Green buys them from orphanages," Cassandra told her. "They work in the machinery with their thin little arms and tiny hands. If they grow up, they end up in the mines or the polishing room with us."

Malvina swallowed hard and held her tongue. Children were a valuable source of labor. They did work adults could not, and sometimes their earnings kept their whole families. She finally gasped for air after the rapid walk and heavy burden.

"White lady wearing a corset," one of the other girls sighed, as if Malvina was the silliest goose in creation and she had been tasked to herd her.

They finally let her sit in a dingy little room with only one rickety wooden stool and a dim cage-like lamp with two coughing pixies in it. Malvina sat to catch her breath and unstrapped the parcels.

"You could be with us a spell," Cassandra said. "Best be comfortable."

It was another couple hours before a pair of messenger pixies came in to see Tashunka. Malvina had counted all her captors and drawn up mental sketches of them for later use. She hadn't decided if they should all hang or be sent west to work on the railroads until they dropped from exhaustion and thirst in the prairie sun.

She watched one of the girls use an ointment from a small pot on Chogan's wounds. The others talked softly or napped. She tried to rest. An alien thought, dark and worrisome, niggled at her. There was no guarantee she would see the sun again. She might very well die down here.

Malvina definitely did not want to die. She wanted...somehow parties and suitors and new dresses all seemed small and petty now. These people lived hard lives, but they were not bored. She didn't want to live that hard of a life, but filling her head with something besides novels and Godey's Lady's Book seemed to appeal. Her father might not approve.

The thought of her father, owner of the local newspaper, made her shiver. He would report this, oh yes. By Daniel Webster and Horace Greeley, he would report this action, and its direct results on his family and in the end, public sentiment would run so high none of the miners or workers would get out alive.

The thought gave her a smile of grim satisfaction, for just a moment, and then dismayed her just as quickly. They had not harmed her in any way since the abduction. They only wanted to be heard.

Malvina kept thinking as the messengers talked to Tashunka. He nodded and occasionally stamped a rear hoof to make a point.

"We will not go and we will not give. Tell them we have Miss Kesler, her chaperone and young Mr. Green. Remind them we are holding them in the mines and any action taken against us will harm them as well." He crumpled the paper and threw it aside.

Malvina considered making a dive for it. She knew she'd never manage, so she slid off the stool and onto the floor. She reached for the paper and uncrumpled it. She rummaged in her reticule and came up with a small pencil she usually used for filling in dance cards. She moved closer under the pixie lantern and began writing on the back of the note. Only after the first two sentences did she stop to read the message.

"Attention saboteurs," it began, "we consider your work stoppage to be a gross act of revolt and disobedience. If you wish to live, you will release the hostages to the authorities at once and give up your leaders. No longer will we endure your rebellion, however, you shall escape with your lives, if not your livelihood."

Malvina turned it back over and kept writing.

"What engrosses you so, Miss?" Chogan asked, startling her. She looked up.

"My father is Cyrus Kesler, editor of the local paper. He will be writing editorials, so I decided to send out one of my own."

"Of how savages, red and black, human and horse, abducted you, held you and scandalized you?"

She saw the mischievous glint in Chogan's eyes and his smile, and knew he was teasing her. "Naughty," she said, sticking out her tongue. She returned to her writing. The pencil had no eraser, so she went slowly and spelled carefully, not wanting to cross anything out and make the editorial messy.

"There," she said, finished at last. The light seemed brighter and she noticed more of the pixies had joined the lantern and some had even alighted in her hair to read as she wrote. "Mr. Tashunka, if this pleases you, have it delivered to the editor of the paper. My father will know my writing."

Tashunka looked it over and read it three times, seeming to search for hidden messages. He smiled at Malvina. "I will bring more paper when I return."

"And a pen, please." She held up the little pencil, worn dull with writing.

Tashunka gave her a nod. "Indeed."

He returned about an hour later with paper and pen, and a smooth board to serve her for a desk. Malvina had been asking questions as she waited and now began writing again. Tashunka went to check his people.

The paper wavered in her vision and a pixie fell on it as she wrote. She picked the creature up and blinked to clear her own eyes. The room had grown very dim. The pixie in her hand went out.

"Gas!" Chogan struggled to gain his feet, but collapsed in an awkward pile. The dozing women in the far corner never stirred.

"Aye, gas." Malvina coughed. She moved closer to the centaur and laid one hand on his side.

"Pixies only go out completely when they die," Chogan managed. The room grew darker as more of the pixies went out.

Malvina tried to stand and found she could not. Her legs would not bear her. She moved closer to Chogan. He wrapped an arm around her as the last pixie darkened and died.

* * *

Tribune Picayune
Editorial regarding the late upheaval at Diversatile Enterprises
by Cyrus Kesler, Editor

It is with heavy heart I pen this to you, the good people of our fair town. In our midst, saboteurs and abolitionists have found a foothold among the slave classes in the factories and mines. They have ceased their labor, taken honest people hostage and presented outrageous demands.

The owners of Diversatile Enterprises have announced they will endure such behavior no longer. They have dealt with the rebels as was proper. Let their fate stand as a warning to the defiant and discontent, to slaves who would overthrow the natural order and workers who would get above themselves. All employers are encouraged to enforce more stringent rules on their laborers, and forbid any fraternization between workers.

Some of you have heard the rumors, and they are true. After their abduction, my own daughter and sister, inculcated and corrupted by contact with Negroes, native tribes and centaurs, threw in their lots with the saboteurs.

The double funeral will be at 1 p.m. Friday at the Presbyterian Church.

The Taste Of Treasure
Kathryn Sullivan

It all began with a frog.

A jeweled frog of gold and silver with two great rubies for eyes, it was an uncommon gift for a king at his coronation. The elves attending the crowning of the Marshking laughed as they passed the group of dwarves. "As if there aren't enough frogs in the marshes," one commented.

The older dwarves scowled, but the Dwarfking's children, a youth of thirty-five years and a lass of twenty, ignored the jibes. They led a small procession on a different path than that of the elves, off to the side of the newly crowned king and queen.

A short time later, the elf prince's conversation with the new queen was interrupted by the littlest Marshprince. "Look, Mama! Look!" He held up the metal frog, its gold and silver tones reflecting those of the small frog embroidered on his tunic.

"How lovely! Your work, Breccia?" the young queen asked the dwarf who trailed after the children.

"Mine and my brother's." Breccia pushed her dark braids back over her shoulder. "Apologies for the interruption, Your Highness." She bowed slightly to the elf, acknowledging his presence before returning her attention to the queen. "Chert and I thought your children might enjoy it."

"It's got a secret," the next youngest princess said, poking at the jewels on the frog's back. The frog's mouth slowly opened to reveal a tiny insect of jewels with wings of golden wires.

"Exquisite work," the Marshking said, joining his family. "We shall treasure this forever." He turned to the elf. "Your gift is greatly valued as well, Your Highness."

The elf prince looked down at the cloak draped over his arm. The queen smiled at him as she took it and held it out to better display. "What beautiful colors!"

"Shielding and concealment spells, correct?" asked the Dwarfking's son as he joined his sister. He stroked his chin, rumpling his wispy beard, and the two dwarves exchanged a look. "Very practical. Our father sent goblets as well." Chert gestured to the receiving line behind the elf. "They should be with the rest of our delegation."

Breccia could not resist a smile as the littlest prince began croaking while his sister opened and closed the frog's mouth. The queen blushed a light green as the elf looked down at them. "Why don't you go show the frog to Lord Drotzon, my dears," she suggested, turning the small royals in the right direction.

"Yes, Mother," the two chorused.

"Be careful not to drop it," the queen added as they started across the room.

"It may look fragile," Chert said, "but it's not. We dwarves know how to make things that last."

While said at a volume normal in a dwarf workshop, his statement also unfortunately fell into one of those lulls in conversations elsewhere. Breccia could hear the distant croaks of the littlest prince as the stillness spread outward from them. She glanced at her brother, who seemed unaware of how loud he was. She turned to the elf prince, wishing desperately that she could remember his name. "Not to imply that elves don't, Your Highness," she said, feeling her face heat.

"Of course not," the elf replied, his expression unreadable.

Chert looked at them in puzzlement. He turned back to the queen. "It won't break if they drop it," he assured her. "They could drop it off the roof and it wouldn't break."

"We'll go mention that to the Crown Princess as well," Breccia said, tugging at her brother's arm.

***

On the way home, Breccia could no longer contain her excitement. "They liked the frog, Chert! They liked it! Father can't call our work frivolous now!"

"He will anyway," Chert responded. "He'll just say, 'My other children are perfectly happy with making the same old things.'" He sighed. "I'm glad you aren't, Breccia."

"Me, too, Chert. It would be lonely being the only one different." She looked ahead at the older dwarves making up their escort and knew their leader Grimder would be making a full report to the Dwarfking.

Chert looked ahead as well. "What was the matter with Prince Tovenhorlee?"

"I think he thought you were criticizing their gift."

"Why? It's not like we're in competition with them. They give a magical gift and we give a nonmagical one." He thumped his armor. "A boring practical one."

Breccia shrugged. "Who can tell with elves?" She thought she heard a distant rustle in the forest, but the older dwarves ahead didn't pause. "Father will have to let our work go as gifts now. Princess Crystel's birthday is coming up in a few months. I think we should finish our butterflies. She likes butterflies. And she already has goblets and a dagger." She bit her lip in thought. "I think we either need to make the wings thinner or find a lighter material. Otherwise they just sit there and flap and look pretty. Which is nice, but I want them to fly."

"Or we can make the wings bigger and have it flap harder."

"Or faster."

In the lead, Grimder sighed and sent a guard to the end of the column to make sure the two youngsters didn't become so lost in their planning that they forgot where they were going. He sent another guard to keep a watch on the elf spying on them.

***

"So I would guess the Marshking wasn't impressed with that... frog," the Dwarfking asked Grimder when the delegation had returned to the mountain.

"He was delighted with it, my lord. So were the queen and their children. He said they would 'treasure' it. And the children began playing with it right away."

"'Treasure', hmm? Not that I would value his idea of treasure." The Dwarfking mused, playing with the braids of his beard. "And I suppose the elves brought some actual treasure?"

"A cloak."

"Eh, one of those." He sighed. "Still, it's more practical than a frog."

"About that, my lord." Grimder looked about the empty throne room, then edged closer to his king. "The elf prince wasn't happy with how much the children were enjoying it. That seemed to bother him."

"Did it, now?" The Dwarfking slowly smiled.

"Aye. By about the third time the children brought it around, showing it to the guests, he backed into his cluster of hangers-on and didn't come out."

The Dwarfking's smile broadened and he leaned back in his throne, adjusting his crown. "I'm ready to see those two now."

***

Breccia and Chert looked at their father in surprise. "No swords?" Chert asked.

"No more armor-forging?" Breccia repeated.

"You may be asked to help out with those when needed, but you can go ahead and make your little frivolous trinkets as well. Or have you run out of ideas?"

"Oh, no, Father," Breccia said with a grin.

Her father frowned. "I was afraid of that." He sighed. "Your older brothers and sisters seem to like making swords and armor and goblets. Why can't you be content with those?"

Because everyone is making them, Breccia wanted to say, but she knew that would only lead back to the old arguments. She kept quiet and elbowed her brother when he started to open his mouth. He closed it, but gave her a reproachful look as he rubbed his ribs.

The Dwarfking looked from one to the other. "Our neighbor's daughter, Princess Crystel, will have a birthday in six months. Do you think you'll have something ready by then?"

"Oh yes, Father," Chert said. "We're already working on it."

***

The two butterflies fluttered the short distance before landing on the princess' outstretched hands. The golden wings flashed in the light as they slowly opened and closed, displaying their elaborate carvings to those close enough to see. The tiny jeweled bodies sparkled as she launched them back into the air. Princess Crystel clapped her hands in delight. "How beautiful!"

The king and queen smiled while the two butterflies looped around them before returning to the princess. Chert and Breccia exchanged delighted glances as the nearby courtiers made pleased and admiring murmurs. The princess placed one butterfly on her shoulder and left another resting on her wrist. Chert handed the two tiny keys on a slender golden chain to the tutor. "When they slow or stop flying, use the key."

The next gift was presented by the elf prince Tovenhorlee. He drew out a long scarf of silken fabric shimmering with butterflies of every shade and pattern.

"How pretty," Princess Crystel murmured.

The prince gestured, and a spell breeze pulled the scarf up to hang in a beam of sunlight like a banner. Courtiers exclaimed as tiny butterflies shimmered in the light streaming through the scarf and fluttered in midair some distance beyond it. "You can hang it wherever you wish to see them," he said, the spell lowering the scarf back down to drape over his outstretched hands. "Hang it in a doorway or window or wear it in your hair. The spell will work whenever sunlight touches it."

Chert and Breccia exchanged glances, then moved through the crowd back to a far wall of the throne room. "It's no secret that she likes butterflies," Chert started.

"Do you think they spied on us?" Breccia asked. "I thought I heard-"

"Oh yes," Grimder said, joining them, "you did and they did. But watch what you say until we return to the mountain."

"Right," Chert said. "This is not a competition."

He looked back at the royal family and was not surprised to see the elf prince watching them. Elves had good hearing and he hadn't bothered to lower his voice. But there was a woman in among the courtiers who was also looking at him. She was dressed in green and red, and though he did not recognize her, he had a faint recollection of seeing her at the Marshking's coronation. As he watched, she turned and studied the elf prince, then looked back at him with a faint smile.

"Breccia, who is that woman?" But when he tried to point her out to his sister, the woman was gone.

***

A few days after the dwarves returned to the mountain, Chert and Breccia entered the Dwarfking's throneroom to find the mysterious woman talking with their father. "Ah, there they are," she said, "the talented makers of golden frogs and butterflies."

Chert eyed her warily as they approached the throne. "You asked for us, Father?"

The Dwarfking nodded. "This wizard has a challenge you two might be interested in."

"I can see the rivalry beginning between elves and dwarves." The woman looked at the Dwarfking. "You know of what I speak." The Dwarfking squirmed as Breccia and Chert watched in amazement. "We can let it built and fester or we can settle it now." The wizard turned toward Breccia and Chert. "I would like you to construct a bird."

Chert was surprised. "A bird? Why?"

"What type?" Breccia asked.

The woman smiled. "Any type you like, though I do want it to fly. I am issuing the same challenge to a certain elf prince. As to why-" she paused, and her smile broadened –"do you not wish to know who is best? This will be a competition. There will be a judge – not I – and that judge's decision will be on which has the right to be called 'Treasure'."

The Dwarfking took a deep breath. "That … would be a great honor. The judge –"

"The judge has great experience in this area." She looked from the Dwarfking to Chert and Breccia. "Are we agreed? Are you willing to compete?"

Chert saw the excitement in Breccia's eyes. They had always dreamed that their items would be deemed Treasure and no longer dismissed as frivolous trinkets. "Oh yes!" they said together.

***

A few months later the challengers met in a mountain meadow midway between the elf and dwarf kingdoms. The elves lined up below the trees on one side, while the Dwarfking and his guards assembled on the other side. Chert and Breccia walked forward to meet the elf prince and the wizard in the middle.

"Where is our judge?" Prince Tovenhorlee asked, looking about the meadow.

The wizard smiled. "You will meet your judge later. Be assured that all tests will be observed closely. Who wishes to begin?"

"I shall." The elf detached a brooch from his cloak. He held it up so that those standing nearby could see that the outline was that of a firebird. Breccia could not be sure if its shimmer was due to jewels or enamel. The prince stepped back and cupped his hands about the pin. Light grew from his hands and rainbows spilled over the sides. A small wind brushed past them to swirl about his hands as well. The multi-colored light formed into long sparkling wings fanning the air, and slowly the construct arose from his hands.

Its shape resembled that of a firebird with long trailing wings and tail, but made of rainbows instead. It began to circle the meadow, soaring over both groups of observers.

The wizard gestured to Breccia and Chert.

Breccia unwrapped the bundle she carried. Their bird did not resemble any particular type. There was a fine balance between the space in the body needed for the gears and springs to enable it to fly and the wingspan needed to lift both it and the jewels necessary for decoration. Chert inserted the tiny key and wound it. He looked at her, and they let it fly.

The alloy they had chosen for the wings and tail shone brilliantly in the sunlight as it flapped. The jewels decorating the body glittered with their own tiny flashes of colors.

The two constructs circled the meadow together for a time. Breccia kept wondering when the judge would appear, but the wizard only stood and waited.

Finally the mechanical bird slowed and dipped down to land. "Stay," the wizard ordered when Chert started to retrieve it. She raised her voice. "Haven't you decided yet?"

A huge sigh came beside them. "But they were so pretty to watch."

A large dragon unfolded itself from concealment amid the boulders and long grasses. The rainbow firebird flitted by, and green scaled jaws snatched it from midair. It chewed thoughtfully, then carefully deposited the brooch before the elf's feet. "Too much air and very little flavor."

It trotted over to where the other bird had landed. "Now this," it declared, with one eye directed back towards Breccia and Chert and the other at the Dwarfking and his guards, "this is Treasure." It wrapped its tongue about the bird and sighed. "Lovely blend of metal and jewels. Can I have it?"

Quest For The Dragon's Scale
M. R. Williamson

Gadritch Brownthum brushed his long, brown hair from his face as he nervously watched the limp directional flag on the bow of his gondola. Appearing to be sixty or so, the heavyset dwarf looked down at Broderick from the helm's seat and said, "A little more air if you please. We don't want to settle too quickly."

Sweat glistened in Broderick Cliffspring's red beard as he pumped a four-foot, makeshift bellows attached to a wood-burning stove. His blue eyes glistened as he watched another dwarf who was now leaning over the side.

"Fifty feet and holdin'," said Boegus Gladling. As the black-bearded dwarf rose up from the side of the willow-wicker gondola, he grumbled, "Dwarves should be in the mines, not up here with the pigeons."

The trim-looking, middle-aged dwarf then picked up a grappling pole and looked back at Gadritch in the helm's seat.

"Off the bellows and find us a clearing," said Gadritch. "We've lost the wind altogether. Get the grapplin' poles and try to keep us out of the trees as we go down. If we wreck this craft we'll have a long walk back to Leachenwood."

"Over there," said Broderick loudly, pointing directly ahead of them. "If we can just pull ourselves around this next big oak, we'll have a clear spot on the other side."

Boegus winced as the hull of the boat-shaped, willow woven gondola scratched its way through the top of the old oak.

"Just a little more," encouraged Gadritch as he leaned from the helm's seat to peer over the side.

"Now!" shouted Broderick, shoving one of the tree's huge limbs away from the stern.

As the limb bounced off the bottom of the gondola, Gadritch nervously tugged on a black rope hanging from the inside of the fig-shaped, blue balloon. Hot air escaped from the top vent as it opened, allowing the craft to settle slowly between the surrounding trees.

"Over the side with a tether rope, Boegus," ordered Gadritch. "Tie us down to somethin' solid."

Immediately dropping his grappling pole, the black-headed dwarf immediately threw the stern tether rope over the side and slid quickly to the ground. Gadritch watched nervously as the fig-shaped balloon slid softly through the smaller limbs, lowering the gondola closer to the ground.

"Over the side, you old, red-bearded spider," shouted Boegus as he watched Broderick inch his way down the bow tether line.

Gadritch shut off the burner, jumped from the helm's seat, and then leaned over the side. "How close are we to where the 'Watcher' is supposed to be?" he asked as softly as he could.

Boegus immediately froze, looking at the captain of the dwarves.

Broderick only smiled as he finished tying off the gondola.

"The whole of Lake Oxbow and the woods between it and Cutoff," he finally answered as he watched Gadritch climb down the ship's rope ladder.

Just as soon as the old dwarf's foot touched the ground, Gadritch looked to Broderick and said, "We'll keep the stove warm all night. If we don't, the balloon will collapse, and with so little room in these trees we'll have a fit getting it back up." He squinted and asked, "And just what do we have to do once we find this wizard's dragon?"

"I'd like to know that, myself." asked Boegus. Then, as he stepped a bit closer to Broderick, he added, "All's we know now is we have a contest between two captains—you and Feathersmore of the Dragon's Oak elves."

"We'll cook a little somethin' before dark sets in," said Broderick through a half-smile. "I'll lay it all out for you two in the morning before breakfast. I don't think the elves have beat us here. We still have a little time on them and if the wind is in our favor tomorrow, we'll beat 'em across the Oxbow also."

"Very well," grumbled Gadritch. "But if I'm not pleased with it, Boegus and me will drop you off and ride the next wind north."

"Agreed then," said Broderick as he began picking up pieces of wood for the cook fire.

* * *

The first light of the next day crept in as quiet as a mouse's sneeze. Boegus, the only one of the three close to being awake, struggled as he wrestled a pine cone from under his blanket. Now, with his stubby fingers imbedded in his beard, he searched for the elusive field mouse that had been pestering him most of the night. Failing once again to find the little critter, he slid his right arm from under the woolen blanket, grabbed another piece of firewood, and tossed it in the coals.

"Merciful dragons!" exclaimed Broderick as a mound of quilts on the far side of the campfire literally became alive with motion. The bulbous-nosed dwarf quickly sat up, rubbed his eyes, and then glared at the mound of blankets that covered Boegus. "Watch them embers!" he grumbled. "They still have life in 'em."

"The gnomish lad's lying," said Boegus as he pushed the blankets from him and then slowly sat up. "The elves are probably laughing at us this very minute. Even if we do find the 'Watcher', who's gonna be fool enough to take one of his scales?"

"How'd you know that?" snapped Boegus as he struggled to his feet.

"We both heard you," replied Gadritch as he slowly struggled from beneath his covers. "That beast's been chasin' you all night long."

"He's not as bad as he looks," mumbled Broderick, "but I just can't get past how he looks." He then looked at Gadritch and added, "We'll find out where the lad lives. The old Wizard Basil has charged the beast with the lad's safe-keeping, so the dragon will be close there somewhere."

"Soooo," quipped Boegus as he looked at Broderick. "If we actually survive the getting of the dragon's scale, what's in it for us?"

"The sword of Kebron," replied Broderick. "It's been in Feathersmore's family for years."

"And if we lose?" asked Gadritch.

Broderick looked out into the woods and then weakly said, "The axe of Cromlin."

"That's your grandfather's," said Gadritch.

"The same," mumbled Broderick, "but I don't intend to lose it."

"Then . . . this creature actually exists," said Boegus weakly.

"He does," answered Broderick. "The gnome, Long Bob, told me himself. He holds a seat on the Board of Elders at the gnomish village of Cutoff. Seems the lad, Yenwolk, got himself in trouble and the dragon had to step in or risk the old wizard's wrath if he got hurt. Choosin' the former, he was seen by at least four gnomes."

"Are we eating in the gondola this morning?" asked Boegus.

"We might better," answered Gadritch. "Early this mornin' I could have sworn I heard riders pass in the night just west of us. That bein' the case, we might have lost our lead."

"Riders!" exclaimed Broderick. As he and the others scrambled to collect their belongings, he mumbled, "The elves should be afoot."

"Not to worry," assured Gadritch. "They have to go 'round the bend of the lake. We'll go straight across and then pick up the Whitestone Trail on the southern side. Then, it shouldn't be that far before we get to Cutoff."

"Done, then," said Broderick. "I'll fire up the furnace while Boegus loads us some more wood. We'll get that willow-wicker ship thing of yours up in the air in no time."

Now, with Broderick on the five-foot bellows, the logs glistened cherry-red as Gadritch kept an eye on how much extra wood Broderick threw into the furnace.

With the craft straining on the ropes, Boegus threw the last handful of wood into the gondola's deck, released the tethers, and ran for the rope ladder. Barely making it, the nimble dwarf scurried up and onto the deck. With hot air pouring from the vents of the stove, the craft lifted quickly from the ground.

"Grab the grappling poles and keep us off the trees," ordered Gadritch. "We've got a good southerly wind and should see Oxbow in no time." He turned to Boegus and said, "Put out the jibs. We want to keep her nose in the right direction."

Boegus scurried to the front of the vessel, looped the safety rope around his waist, and edged out onto the nose of the gondola. Pulling at a rope attached to the bow, two triangular sails unfurled from the short, horizontal mast protruding from the nose of the ship. The bow of the gondola slowly corrected itself, pointing in the direction the craft was moving.

"There it is!" exclaimed Broderick as the gondola rose well above the trees. But then, Broderick remained strangely quiet, with his eyes transfixed on something in the distance.

Noting that the dwarf captain had obviously spotted something, Gadritch slipped from the helm's seat, eased around the furnace, and joined him. "See somethin'?" he asked.

"Indeed," answered Broderick as he pointed toward the Oxbow Lake. "There's a two-masted ship moving away from the banks. It doesn't have a single sail down, yet it's making an impressive wake." Broderick looked at Gadritch and added, "How could that be? Are the elves using magic?"

Gadritch then quickly turned to Boegus and said, "Get into that helm's seat and watch our direction."

"I can't operate this thing," complained Boegus as he climbed into the tall seat.

"How hard could it be with only three ropes?" shouted Gadritch. "Pull the green one on the right and it'll open the left vent a bit. That'll push us gently to the right. Pull the red one and we'll go left. But whatever you do, don't touch the black one. It opens the top vent and we'll sink like a rock."

"Right one attached to the left and we go right, but left one hooked to the right one and we go left and..." Boegus rolled his eyes and pulled his hands away from the rope's wooden handles altogether.

Gadritch then looked back at what Broderick was still puzzling over. "Well, that is a riddle," he quipped. "Certainly some kind of ship. No sail, but it's still moving fast enough to give us trouble."

"You're the machinist here," said Broderick. "You've made things of black iron, oak wood, and the elfin, white metal. Now tell me just what kind of vessel moves without wind or paddle."

"An elfin one," answered Gadritch as he pointed out the flag atop the first mast.

"A white unicorn on a field of dark blue," said Broderick weakly. "It's Feathersmore all right. He's cheating again."

"He's spelled the whole darned ship," shouted Boegus as he all but stood in the helm's seat.

"Calm down, Boegus, and pull on that red rope just a little bit. You're letting us drift too far to the right."

Little by little, a smile worked its way beneath Gadritch's big, bulbous nose as they closed the distance between them and the ship. "I see it," he replied just above a whisper. "They have a chimney, and they're burnin' oak wood and boilin' water. Steam's pushin' that thing."

"Steam?" quizzed Broderick.

"Certainly. See those wheels turnin' on each side of the ship? There's at least a dozen paddles spinnin' on an axle and it's bein' turned by steam some kind of way."

"I don't get it," complained Broderick. "I still think it's spelled."

"No, no, no," corrected Gadritch. "It's like you breathin', in and out. The steam off the boilin' water is your breath in. When the machine breathes that steam out, it pushes on a plunger and lever system that turns the axle and spins them paddles."

"Well it's spinnin' pretty good," said Boegus. "Plus, they've just dropped a sail to boot and we've all but stopped gainin' on them."

"Spotted us," said Gadritch as he spun around, trotted around the furnace, and then ordered, "Get down, Boegus. This simply won't do."

Now, with the elfin vessel taking a more easterly course on the crescent-shaped lake, Gadritch steered straight south.

"I believe we got 'em," said Gadritch. "We'll cut across the woods in the middle of the lake's curve. I believe we'll beat 'em to the southern banks. Then, they'll be afoot in the forests between the lake and Cutoff. Now, one of you get to the bow of this thing and help me spot the Whitestone Road when we make the southern banks."

Boegus eased past the helm's seat, slowed, and then looked up at Gadritch. "But are not those woods south of the Oxbow Lake where the dragon stays?"

Gadritch quickly looked at Broderick, who was slowly shaking his head.

"Maybe," admitted the dwarf captain, "but then again, maybe not. I 'spect the old wizard will have him a bit closer to the boy. He, his mother, and some friends saw him at a place called Sugar Creek Springs. That's a bit south of the Cutoff and quite near his own home I suppose. The old Wizard's son, Benjamin, told me that Yenwolk actually talked to the creature in those woods just behind his home."

"Talked!" exclaimed Gadritch. "How is it that he'll talk to gnomes and not to dwarves anyways?"

Boegus looked disgustedly at Broderick and then added, "Do you blame him? It once was that every time any kind of dragon flew over Leachenwood's entrance one of Broderick's hard-heads would turn loose one of those big swing-bows at him. It took the old Wizard Basil, himself, to threaten to seal the entrance of the caverns to get 'um to quit."

"Ohhh," grumbled Broderick. "That's in the past. The wizards and me got an agreement. Now, Benjamin and I are just like . . ." The dwarf captain tried to cross his stubby fingers on his right hand. In failing to do so, he said, "We're real close anyways."

"Hope so," mumbled Boegus. "Dragons are dragons, and they have long memories." Boegus then looked to the port side of the vessel and exclaimed, "We got 'em! We got 'em! We're over the Oxbow again and the elves are just breakin' 'round the point."

"Just what I expected," said Gadritch as he stood from his helm's seat. "Now get to the bow. We'll be over the Cutoff woods before you know it, and be looking for that wizard's beast too. Bright yellow and green should stand out down there."

"He won't even see us comin'" added Broderick. "Dragons don't have enemies so they hardly ever feel the need to look up."

Gadritch slowly closed the damper on the stove allowing his craft to settle closer to the tops of the trees. "Lay off the bellows, Broderick," he whispered. "All that huffin' and puffin' is sure to attract his attention."

"We're not that far from the Cutoff Road," whispered Broderick as he joined Boegus on the bow. "I can see smoke from the village just off the starboard bow. Sugar creek should be dead ahead."

The huge, blue dirigible drifted over the Cutoff road as quiet as an owl's wings. What few gnomes they noticed never bothered to look up. Gadritch chuckled from the helm's seat, completely amused at the accomplishment. Then, as the breeze took them back into the woods south of the road, it soon became quite obvious that some dwarves hardly look up either.

"What the devil is that?" exclaimed Gadritch as the gondola shook violently. The old dwarf struggled to keep from being thrown from the helm's seat.

The lurch was so violent it sent Broderick and Boegus tumbling to the deck. Then, as the vessel lurched again, a noise came more sickening than any stomachache—the sound of ripping canvass.

"It's like we hit somethin'," said Boegus, "but we're a good fifty feet above the tallest tree."

"On the bellows, Boegus!" shouted Gadritch. Then, as he opened the dampers as wide as possible, he looked up into the fig-shaped balloon. "We got a huge, six-foot hole right at the top vent! Throw some wood in this thing, Broderick. If we don't get the heat up in a hurry, we're gonna drop like ship's anchor."

"But . . . but, he's not here," said Boegus weakly as he rushed to look down from the port side of the vessel. "We need to put down right now and look for him. Broderick!" he shouted down into the forest.

"Ha!" exclaimed Gadritch loudly. "That's exactly what we're doing. Now pump that bellows or we'll crack 'er up entirely."

* * *

As Boegus frantically pumped the bellows of their 'sinking' ship, Broderick found himself out of the gondola and clinging to one of the top limbs of a huge white oak.

"A fine mess I'm in," he grumbled as he dangled beneath the huge limb.

Having a bit of trouble maintaining his hold on the tree, he looked toward the body of the old oak. It was larger than the waist of three men.

"Just wonderful," he mumbled, "I'll never get a grip around that. Now, just how do I work this out without breakin' bones?"

"Not with a crossbow," spoke someone from the ground directly below him.

From the sound of the deep, guttural tone, the dwarf captain knew it was something other than gnomish. With his eyes all but shut, Broderick tried to maintain his grip on the limb. Finally, realizing his hopeless situation, he worked up the nerve to look down.

"Valerie take me now," he said weakly as he looked at the creature lying in the leaves below him. His forehands were three times that of any man's hands, and his length, tail and all, had to be thirty-five feet at the least.

Noticing the dragon's bright, yellow eyes, the dwarf looked away, closed his eyes, and then pushed his forehead against the limb he was hugging.

"Praying to the old oak will not help you there, Master Dwarf," spoke the voice again. "There are no big limbs between you and I. Just turn loose of the oak. I will catch you."

Hearing no anger in the beast's voice, the dwarf looked down once again. Then, trying to ignore the huge, black claws of the creature, Broderick tried to speak, but his mouth was so dry he could hardly make a good start.

"You have me at a disadvantage, Sir," he finally got out. "If I am to die here, I would at least like to know your name."

"I know your name," responded the dragon. "I heard it shouted from that thing you were last in. The Wizard Benjamin has spoken of you in a favorable way. Sooo . . ." The dragon slowly pushed himself up on his haunches, looked up, and then continued, "The only thing that needs be done now is to change your opinion of me."

"You will not harm me?" asked the dwarf.

The dragon sighed heavily as he looked away from the dwarf and into the dark of the woods. Then, he finally said, "You will fall into my hands eventually, Master Dwarf. It will mean much more to me if you do it on faith than have it happen after your strength fails. After all, if I had wanted you dead, I would have caught you on the way to the tree you are now gripping."

Broderick slowly shook his head. "I see your point, Sir. Are you ready?"

"More than you, obviously," responded the dragon impatiently.

The dwarf then closed his eyes, took as deep a breath as possible, and then released his grip on the limb. The wind whistled by his ears. Leaves, acorns, and small limbs stung his neck and back as he fell. But when he hit, it was as if he fell into his own goose-down mattress.

"You can open your eyes now," spoke the dragon as he gazed amused at the being now cupped in his hands.

The dwarf slowly peeped up through his fingers at the one holding him. Following the yellow scales up the underside of the beast's chin, his eyes just could not get past the creature's teeth. They were meshed together like the veins of a feather. The dragon then lowered his forehands and sat the dwarf in the leaves in front of him.

"Thank you, Sir," said Broderick as he struggled to his feet. "I owe you. If it weren't for you, this might have been the end of me."

"You are a friend of Benjamin. You can repay me by making a friend of the boy Yenwolk. I heard you speak of him as I followed above your craft."

"Tell me," said the dwarf. "Do your scales ever itch?"

The dragon pushed himself up a bit straighter, looked down at the dwarf, and then said, "What sort of a question is that? Do your fingernails ever itch?"

"Well, no, not really," answered Broderick. He then asked just above a whisper, "Then, it would probably hurt to pull one for someone wouldn't it?"

"It wouldn't feel good," replied the dragon as he squinted his eyes at the dwarf. "Just what are you up to? A group of elves are also a bit south of here and in equally as big a hurry."

"We . . . Uh . . .are looking for the one who watches the boy, Yenwolk."

"You seek the Wizard Benjamin's dragon," replied the creature. "You seek Pandahar."

"Yes. The one who watches the young gnome."

"And just what part does this scale play?" asked the dragon suspiciously.

The dwarf marveled at the intelligence of the creature sitting before him, looked into the woods, and then sighed heavily. "Proof we saw him," he finally got out.

The huge creature slowly shook his head, raised himself from the ground, and then backed up a bit.

"I will not play your game," he added as he stretched his wings out and shook them. "Seek the boy who is watched. He has your proof, but it should cost you. He got it from me."

Then, in a flurry of leaves and pine needles, the great-winged, forest dragon leapt into the air. The canopy hardly moved as the huge creature slipped between the trees to disappear above their limbs.

Broderick sat down hard on the leaves and rubbed his face briskly. "Merciful dragons," he said through a heavy sigh. "I thought I was a goner," he added weakly as he looked back up to where he last saw what the gnomes called 'The Pan'.

The snickering in the scrub just south of him then made him realize he still wasn't alone.

"Boegus, you black-bearded hobbit. Is the vessel in one piece?" he grumbled.

"Yes, but it's jus' like you—down, in shock, and too weak to stand," replied the dwarf as he stepped from the bushes.

"Very funny," grumbled Broderick as he struggled to his feet. "What did we hit?"

"Not sure, but whatever it was will keep Gadritch sewing for a while. He said he'd repair the thing while we go to the village and find that boy."

"Good," replied Broderick. Then, as he looked toward the east, he added, "We're a little south of the Cutoff Road and probably real close to his house." He then stepped a bit closer to Boegus and said through a little grin, "The 'Watcher' saved my bacon. He also told me that young Yen has one of his scales. If Feathersmore knows this also, the race is truly on. We need to get to the road and talk to the first gnome we come across. That's the only way I know to find where the lad lives."

* * *

It wasn't long until it became obvious that Broderick was right. As they drew near the rear of a little cabin, he waved at a young girl working in her garden.

"Good day to you," he called.

She paused, wiped the sweat from her brow, and leaned on her hoe. Brushing her long, brown hair from her forehead, she held the smile and replied, "I thought the dwarf village was to the north."

Boegus grinned. "Ahhh yes, Leachenwood," he quipped. "It is, but we took a shortcut. Could you tell us where the Stonesmith cabin is? We're looking for the lad, Yenwolk."

"Right there," she answered, pointing to a cabin and barn not more than a hundred yards east of them. "I'm Belinda Pragen. The Stonesmiths are our best friends. They've had lots of visitors this year. I've seen elves also. There's even a group of them there now. I noticed them ride across the road from the lake just minutes before you came up."

"Elves!" exclaimed Boegus.

"Ride?" asked Broderick. "How in this mother's son did they come by horses?"

Boegus shrugged his shoulders. "They're the only somebody's who can summon mounts up from the forest with but a whistle."

"Thank you for your time," said Broderick as he quickly nodded to Belinda, turned to Boegus, and then said, "We must go. It may be that they don't know what the young gnome holds."

As they walked briskly through the garden between the two homes, Boegus pointed toward the cabin. "There they are," he said just above a whisper. "I can see a couple of their horses tied on the far side of the house."

"Magic," grumbled Broderick. "Feathersmore cheated. Somehow, I know they all cheated."

"Did you say they couldn't use magic?" asked Boegus, watching his friend's expression closely.

"Not sure," grumbled Broderick as they stepped from the garden. Then, as the two entered the yard, Broderick slowed abruptly, holding Boegus back also.

"What have you spotted?" whispered Boegus, noting the uncomfortable look on the captain's face.

"It's him," replied Broderick weakly.

"Who's him?" asked Boegus, noting there were several on the front porch.

Finally, Boegus' eyes grew wide as he spotted the old, white-bearded fellow in a chair on the far side of the porch.

"Basil," he said weakly. "What'll we do?"

"Just keep coming," spoke the old fellow loudly as he stood from the chair.

A bit stooped, and well under six feet tall, the old dwarf looked almost frail compared to the others as he slowly worked his way through them. The breeze gently blew his thinning white hair from his face as he stepped from the porch. Dressed in a beige robe trimmed in crimson, he leaned upon a staff that looked older than he was, but he still looked every bit a wizard.

"Find what you've been looking for?" he asked.

His pale, blue eyes sparkled with clarity uncommon for his age as he searched the dwarves' expressions for a clue most others would miss.

Noting Feathersmore and the other elves were grinning, Broderick replied, "Yes . . . and no Sir."

Knowing that Old Basil wasn't the most patient of the Alvis family, Boegus grimaced, and then rubbed his face briskly.

Little by little, a smile formed on the face of the old wizard as Yenwolk eased to his side.

"What to do?" asked the Wizard Basil as he looked down at the young gnome.

"They want the same thing," said Yenwolk. "It's like some kind of game to them."

"Game..." The old one mused the situation as he watched to two dwarves squirm. He looked at Feathersmore and said, "Join us." Then, turning back to Yenwolk, he said, "Let me have what they seek."

The wizard took the scale and held it in his open hand in front of them. "This was presented to the lad by the 'Watcher' to prove to others of his existence," he explained. "Pandahar, or The Pan as my son calls him, is under a charge to protect the lad until he becomes of age." His face then clouded up as he pointed a crooked finger at Feathersmore and Broderick and said, "You two would distract him from that with your pointless, little pursuit."

Then, as the two watched, the scale in his hand split in twain.

"You may take you each a piece," he instructed. "You now have two choices. I will set my dragon, Doppelganger, between the Cutoff and the Oxbow Lake. If either of you get past him and are still able to hold the object, you will win his prize."

"That could be a great deal," whispered Boegus as Feathersmore slowly shook his head.

"We know your red dragon," said Broderick. "He doesn't play well with others. What is the other choice?"

"Give what you would have won to the Stonesmith family," he answered without hesitation.

"Auugh!" groaned Broderick as he turned and looked toward Belinda's garden.

"Unfair, Broderick?" asked Basil. "Perhaps you would like to play with my dragon on your way back to the lake," added the old fellow as he held the halves a bit closer to the dwarf.

With the thought of what Doppelganger had done in the past when Basil was young, Broderick slowly turned, faced the old wizard, and then asked, "Would a price of silver do as well?"

"Well," quipped the wizard as he looked down at Yenwolk. "What do you think?"

"Not sure, Sir," responded Yen. "I wouldn't want to spoil a friendship with the elves or the dwarves."

"Well put, my puzzling, young friend," responded Basil. Then, as he looked back up at the two, he added, "My 'game' is not of the lad's doing and I don't expect any hard feelings toward him. How does three, one-ounce ingots sound?"

"Auugh!" complained Broderick again as he watched Feathersmore and the other elves quickly search their pockets. Then, looking at the scale pieces still held out in the old wizard's hand, he slowly took out his pouch, fished out the required amount, and then handed it to the young gnome.

"Take it," encouraged Basil, noting that Yen was hesitating. "A wizard never refuses a rightful gratuity. These two would have sport with a creature that clearly had his forehands full already. But, all in all, they have learned a most valuable lesson--never vex a wizard, especially one from the Whitestone Castle."

A Bit Of A Bind
CRS Bailey

Corsets shape the chest, restrict the waist, and discourage deep breathing. The last is more of a side-effect, but it was the problem that Samiel was focusing on with intense irritation.

He did not like corsets – he did not like anything about his current costume, but the corset was the worst – and he really did not like being unable to breathe. The next time he saw his father, Magelord Hartley, he would be sure to express his displeasure noisily, possibly violently, depending on how long he was forced to continue this ruse of being a human girl instead of a half-elf boy.

"Samantha, sit up," Aileen Fagan hissed. Samiel's nursemaid enjoyed the temporary promotion to "aunt" a little too much; it meant Sam had far less room to call her out for being imperious and acting above her station. "You'll ruin your dress!"

Perhaps that was the plan, Sam thought mutinously, but said nothing, only scowling.

"Don't look so dour. You're supposed to be the very example of maidenhood." Aileen could almost manage a straight face when she said that. "Which means you should smile."

"How can I smile when I can barely breathe?" Sam huffed.

"Now you know how I feel every day," Aileen said haughtily.

Sam rolled his eyes. "You hate corsets, too. Yours isn't nearly as tightly laced as mine!"

"I'm not exactly looking for a husband," Aileen said, waving aside the insult to her weight and fortitude.

"*Neither am I*," Sam barely avoided screaming.

"But you're supposed to look like a young lady, and a young lady would naturally be searching for a husband if she came to Metropolita like this, without one."

A young lady was not allowed the fidgets of a young man – Samiel had gotten some smart raps on his knuckles for forgetting that earlier in the airship ride, so he wasn't about to forget it now. He toyed with the chestnut brown wig's ringlets and wished he could tug on his own short, dirty blond hair, or wipe the sweat off his forehead with his sleeve. It was infernally hot in this getup, especially with the wig. The airship went so high that even the deck was enclosed, to make sure the cabin had enough oxygen. Samiel just wished that oxygen was cooler, though the coal-burning engines meant the ship would be overly warm even in the dead of winter, much less in this wretched summer heat.

"Stop squirming," Aileen ordered. "If you must wriggle, do yourself some good and use your fan."

The fan! Sam had forgotten it entirely, half on purpose. It was pink and white, made of delicate, fancy woods, edged with lace. It wasn't the best for a cooling breeze, but it did stir the air. More to the point, it meant he could speak a little more freely.

Even here, in this cramped, hot cabin, they had to be wary about dwarf spies listening at keyholes, or through mechanized contraptions they had no knowledge of. The fan code had been worked out well in advance of the trip. Sam used his opening of the fan mostly to make obscene comments about the heat, things that no lady would dare say aloud.

Aileen smiled but hid it with her fan, telling him to control his temper.

His finger traced the side rib of the fan and he held it to the left of his face as he fluttered it quickly. Another vile statement, this one about Aileen's weight. Her eyes narrowed, and she snapped her fan shut and smacked it into her left palm.

Don't waste my time, she meant.

Two taps to the base of his fan and a soft swipe at his brow with a handkerchief, among other flapping motions. *You are loyal to my father. I am only obligated to him.*

She sighed and opened her fan again, slowly. She held it low in her lap as she fanned herself. *It is for the best.*

Sam fiddled with an eardrop. The subtle points of his ears were hidden by the wig, but young ladies naturally needed jewelry, even if it only drew attention to the thing he most needed to hide. *It's for elves.* He tapped the earring before moving his hand away, letting it arc towards Aileen before resting it in his lap. *You're human.*

Aileen loudly drummed her fingers on the bench and crossed her legs, smacking her lips a little. *It's to end this* stupid *war.*

He mopped at the sweat gathering on the back of his neck, fanning it as he lifted the curls away from his skin. *Why me?*

Her handkerchief moved across her own brow and she fluttered her eyelashes. *Your father trusts no one else.*

He dug a book out and started reading, ignoring Aileen and the flush of pride at her coded words. His human mother had abandoned him after less than a month, unable to tolerate a baby that didn't cry or coo. Magic had restored his speech, magic his mother had insisted father not use, but when she left, there was no reason not to use the spell. Sometimes he fancied it was the spell that made his voice soft and feminine; perhaps father had failed to cast it correctly. The rest of the time, he blamed his elven heritage. Either way, it was his father's fault, he supposed.

The intercom crackled to life. "We will be setting down in Metropolita in twenty minutes. Please remain seated for the duration of the landing."

Sam sighed in relief. At least in Metropolita there was a chance of a breeze! He'd thought getting a private cabin with just Aileen would be a blessing, but it couldn't even be called quiet, it was so near the engines – meaning there was also no view to speak of, except what they could see of the hallway when they raised the blind on the door.

Landing was ten minutes of being jostled about the small cabin, clinging to the bench to avoid a concussion. A dwarf crewman came by to offer assistance with their bags, and needed to call over a friend to maneuver Sam's steamer trunk off the boat. Sam and Aileen carried a pair of small valises each, and it was from Aileen's purse (filled with Magelord Hartley's money, of course) that the dwarves were paid for their help. Aileen's husband Clem spotted them by merit of being twice as tall as most of the dwarf-crowd at the docks. He had brought a horse and carriage, and a footman besides. Sam relaxed. The footman helped Clem load the luggage and the "ladies" climbed into another stuffy box, though at least this one had working windows so they could catch a hint of a breeze. Clem got in after them, clasping his wife's hands with a broad grin.

"I've missed ye so, dearie," he said, kissing her sweetly. Sam rolled his eyes. "And how is my bonnie lass?" he turned to Sam.

"Dying of heatstroke," Samiel sulked. "And *suffocation*," he added, leveling a glare at Aileen.

"Here, I brought some water. I remember my own trip on the blasted thing," Clem said helpfully, offering Sam a flask. It wasn't cold, but it was sweet and clear; he drank from it in large gulps. He poured some on his handkerchief and left the dripping cloth on his neck. Aileen gave him a disapproving look that he ignored.

"We're almost t' the apartments," Clem said. He closed the curtains but left the windows open. "Nothin' unexpected on the journey over?" he asked, and the words were so heavy with meaning that Sam twitched, uncomfortable at how obvious Clem was even when trying to be subtle.

"Honestly, Daddy, what could possibly have happened?" he asked, with a pointed smile, eyes flicking to the curtains as they swayed with the movements of the carriage. "It was a perfectly boring journey." He crossed his legs in that ladylike way that pinched something awful but was apparently required.

Aileen chortled, patting Clem on the thigh. "She says that, but she stayed up on the deck as long as the captain would let her. I think she rather enjoyed her first airship ride."

"And he sent me back down when the view was finally getting interesting." Sam shook his head. "At least on deck there was room to breathe!"

The carriage rumbled to a stop. "Here we are!" Clem bellowed, opening the door and helping the "ladies" back out. Sam looked up – and up, and up, and up. He'd never seen a building so tall – it had to be at least ten stories! "We're on the top floor," Clem said cheerfully. A doorman in blue livery stepped forward to help Clem and the footman with the luggage.

Sam cringed. "We have to walk up *how* many flights of stairs with that trunk?"

"Stairs! Of course not, milady," the doorman scoffed. "We've had a pneumatic lift since Greely Towers were built! Just follow me, ladies and gentlemen." The footman didn't seem terribly impressed at his promotion to "gentleman."

Gleaming reflections from white-pink marble floors and brass fixtures half-blinded Sam once the doors were open. Greely Towers was lit with electricity, far brighter than candles, even brighter than oil lamps. The cloudless day outside had been dimmer! The doorman led to a brass gate and pulled on a rope. With a frightful hissing and sucking noise, the empty cavern beyond the gate filled with a small chamber. A young dwarf in the same blue livery smiled cheerfully at them. The doors opened – first the brass gates, then glass doors behind them.

"Step in, all who's going up," the dwarf chirped. All but the doorman got on. "What floor?"

"Eleven," Clem answered.

The glass doors closed with another sucking noise, and the gates beyond them rattled back together. The doorman waved and turned to walk away. The lift-dwarf pulled a few levers. "Floor eleven!" The hissing was much louder inside, and it gave Sam the shivers. Black-brass-black-brass flashed by beyond the glass doors as floors whizzed past. Then they jerked to a stop. "Floor eleven, there you are," the dwarf said. The gate and the doors parted and they stumbled out.

Sam felt faint. He'd gone up ten floors in less than ten seconds. Maybe it was altitude sickness. Aileen didn't look well, either.

"It was a frightful long journey for my poor girls, wasn't it?" Clem shook his head. "Let's get to the rooms and you can have a rest." He and the footman picked up the trunk and walked along the hall. They stopped at room 1193, what felt like a whole city block away from the lift. Sam stumbled in and was perfectly prepared to fall asleep even with the corset on.

Aileen sat him down in the little parlor, though.

Once the trunk was installed and the footman gone, Clem and Aileen sat at the table across from Sam. Clem pulled papers out of a case and spread them around.

"The thrust of the ruse is I'm a wealthy gentleman farmer from elf-country come in to find my lass a good lad of my own stock, get her mind off of adderpated elf-boys. It so happens the Mayor of Metropolita is human and has a son of an age with Sam, and many of his mates are of good family and fortune," Clem started. "Papers establishing intent, verifying identity, right to cross borders, they're all here. Fortunately, just yesterday I got the last piece we needed." He tapped a square of parchment, decorated with gold leaf. "Unfortunately, the Mayor is more interested in seeing if my daughter is worthy than inviting a boor like me to a dance. It's a provisional invitation. First, we go to dinner at the vice mayor's home tonight. If he signs the ticket, you'll attend the dance in the company of his family. If he doesn't, we may as well go home."

"Tonight?" Sam said weakly.

"You have an hour to rest and two to prepare," Aileen decided. She hustled him into the bedroom and started helping him out of the difficult clothes and wig. A nightgown was tugged over his head and he was shoved under the coverlet.

Despite the rough treatment, it was easy to fall asleep. The bed was so comfortable…

But it couldn't last long, of course. Aileen dragged him back out all too soon, stuffing him into a different dress, this one made from jade-colored silk, with sage-green embroidery and gold buttons. The corset felt a hair looser, but that was the only positive thing he had to say about the outfit. The white, low-heeled boots were alright, he supposed.

Aileen had worked on the wig while he was asleep. It looked positively elegant, though he was less impressed when it was on him. She attacked his face with paints and powders and scents.

"It'll be just the two of us going," Clem explained. He was already in a smart tailcoat, and was knotting his tie. He looked like a fat black cat with two tails. "Aileen will have been too tired." Aileen did not look too tired, but Sam was glad his taskmaster would be staying home.

They rang the bell and the dwarf brought the lift up for them again. Going down bothered Sam a bit less. The carriage took them much farther than the docks this time.

The pair of them stayed silent, aside from Clem's wet, rattling snores. Samiel was too anxious to sleep, and the carriage ride wasn't really long enough to allow it. Clem woke when they stopped, snorting and coughing. He peered out the window before the footman got the door open.

"Vice Mayor H. Warton Gilmour's residence, sah," he said, giving Sam a hand to get down from the coach. Clem took Sam's arm gently and walked him up to the door. He knocked loudly. Clem did most things loudly.

The door creaked open, but Sam didn't see who answered it. He heard a little gasp and looked down.

"You're pretty! Are you an angel?" a small girl asked, eyes wide. Sam flushed.

"No, I'm not an angel," he mumbled, embarrassed. Pretty! Most girls would be happy with such an honest compliment, but Samiel would have preferred to be called mannish, if his looks had to be remarked upon in this getup.

"She's my little angel," Clem corrected, kissing Samiel's brow. "An' what's your name, poppet?"

The girl beamed. "I'm Annaliese Mayhew Gilmour!" She started to say some more, but a nursemaid scooped her up.

"Annaliese, you're not to answer the door!" she scolded. "I'm sorry, sir, milady. Did she disturb you?"

"Not at all," Clem said. "My name is Clyburn Davy, and this is my daughter Samantha." Sam curtsied, and the nurse did as well (deeper and more gracefully).

"The Master is expecting you," the nurse said, and she led them into the house. The dining room was large – too large for the number of chairs at the table. A golden chandelier dangled above, lit with electricity like Greely Towers.

A finely dressed man came in another door. He was smiling broadly, and he clapped Clem on the shoulder. "Mr. Davy, good to see you again – and this must be your lovely daughter....Amanda?"

"Samantha," Sam corrected, with what was hopefully a polite, obliging smile, instead of a grimace.

"Of course, of course. A pleasure to meet you, Samantha," he said, kissing Sam's hand. "I am Vice Mayor H. Warton Gilmour."

"Mr. Gilmour," Sam said with a curtsy.

"And here are my children," Gilmour announced, as three young men and two young ladies entered the room, with a matronly women bringing up the rear. "And my dearest Phoebe." His wife beamed at him. "Laura, Patsy, Owen, Leslie, and Isaiah, these are the Davys, Samantha and Clyburn. And I believe Annaliese has introduced herself already, she usually does." Annaliese smiled broadly at her father, who chuckled. Bows and curtsies all around and then they could sit for dinner.

Over the course of the meal, Sam was told no less than ten times that he was pretty, usually by Isaiah, the youngest boy, who claimed to be "nearly" fifteen. Owen stared at Sam as if he'd hung the moon, and Leslie nearly dropped anything he was asked to pass to "Samantha." The girls tittered but also seemed a bit in awe of Sam.

Sam tried to remember everything Aileen had said to do (or mostly what she'd said *not* to do, which was a lot). Don't be shy but don't speak too much. Be witty but not too funny and certainly not too clever but don't be stupid either. Don't ask about anything you really want to know about, focus on the lives of the people you're meeting, what they would want to brag of. He got Mr. Gilmour talking about golf, Owen talking about his studies, and Leslie soon followed about his new bicycle. Isaiah blushed and stammered as he talked about all his mates and the things they did for a lark. He'd probably said more than was good for him; some of his more mischievous adventures had gotten him the hairy eyeball from his father.

"Samantha, will you go to the ball with me?" Owen asked, his voice husky.

He blinked, looked at Clem, looked at the plate, and looked back at Owen. "Ball?"

"The City Centennial. The Mayor's hosting a ball, tomorrow night. Come with us. Dance with me?" he asked hopefully.

"Ah, of course," Sam faked a smile. "Certainly."

* * *

Another day, another corset. Samiel wanted desperately to be home. Owen Gilmour picked him up at seven on the dot in the family carriage, with the rest of the family piled in. Well. Not all the rest, just the ones over sixteen, which at least meant no Isaiah and no Annaliese or Patsy. Owen appeared to be on the verge of holding Sam's hand the whole ride.

The Mayoral Estate was rather small and quaint in comparison to Magelord Hartley's tower. Sam held Owen's arm on the walk up the stairs, letting him lead Sam into the dance hall.

"May I?" Owen asked. He was so nervous he was almost shaking.

"Er – "

"Who's your friend, Owen?" A young man draped his arm around Owen's shoulders. "And why haven't I met such a lovely lady as yourself, miss?"

"I'm new in town. Just got in yesterday," Sam answered. "And you are?"

"Leopold Yates. My father's the mayor."

"Leo, I was just about to ask Miss Davy t-to dance."

"Then allow me claim her for the second dance," Leo beamed. Owen nudged him, red in the face.

"I refuse," Sam said, arching an eyebrow. "Owen, you absolutely may. Shall we?" he offered his hand. Aileen would have been appalled, but Samiel knew this lad's type, the ones who had every girl after just a pretty smile. They only really wanted the girl who ran the other way.

"Wha-?"

"Next time you ask a lady to dance, Mr. Yates, try actually *asking*," Sam scolded.

It was three dances before Leo came back, flushed with embarrassment. "Alright. Please do me the honor of dancing with me?" he asked, with a half-bow.

"Better," Sam said, like he would pat a dog for repeating an old trick. "More sincerely?"

"Honestly! …Miss Davy. May I have this dance?"

"Yes," Sam smiled, and Leo beamed again, swooping him off to the dance floor. It was a lively step that brought them chest-to-chest. Sam had noticed the military uniform on him, but it was only in brushing against Leo that Sam paid attention to the medals.

"Have you been in the military long?" he asked.

"A year or so. This is my first leave home."

"Why do you fight for the dwarves? Their race war with the elves is not a human concern."

"Look around you," Leo said, leaning in close to let a pair of dwarf dancers pass by. "Metropolita is a city of many races. Dwarf-country is not about height. They want only to know that you are willing to work, no matter what that work may be, as long as it benefits the society. In elf-country, humans can only be servants, but here…my father was elected mayor, by the whole city, not just dwarves or humans. Elves don't even vote except in their closed-door councils. A common human has no power in their society."

"My father – " Sam started, meaning quite the wrong male when he first opened his mouth, but fortunately Leo cut him off before he could dig himself into trouble.

"May have the wealth of his land, but if the elves decided to take that land, who would stop them?" Leo said harshly. "He has no title, no people, no real strength. He knows that if you married elf-kind you would be subjugated, so he takes you here, where you can meet a real man who has not lived under the boot-heels of the fair folk so long he has forgotten how to stand."

"You mean a young hot blood like you?" Sam sneered derisively. "You're still a boy. and you may have seen combat but it hasn't made a man of you. I bet you're still just foot soldier fodder for the dwarvish generals who throw your type on elvish pikes."

Leo's hands gripped Sam hard, and his voice was furious but quiet as he leaned in again. "I am a lieutenant commander, which means not only do I know the movements of the army. I assist with planning them. After our leave, my unit will teach elvendom the true power of dwarven and human ingenuity."

"What do you mean?" Sam asked, staying still and calm because his mission and possibly his life depended on convincing Leo he was giving in.

"The war will be won with new weapons. Magics cannot stop them. A single one dropped from an airship could destroy an entire city."

"But elves do not build cities," Sam said softly.

"No. Humans do. And humans are making the supplies for the elven army, are they not? Textile work, that's beneath elves, isn't it? Mass-producing weapons offends their little craftsman souls, but they'll use what's cheap and available if they have to, so humans make the weapons, too. Am I wrong? Rivertown, Lakewell, Harbortown; they all craft for the army."

"You would attack your own kind?"

"I would show them that serving elves forever does them no favors," he corrected.

"…by attacking them."

Leo laughed, but it was quiet and not particularly joyful. "We need only destroy an adequate amount of the elves' precious forests, and the humans will think to themselves that four cities could fit in that ruined forest, and perhaps the weapon could destroy their homes as well. I do not wish to kill, but I refuse to die or lose rights because my ears aren't sharp enough."

* * *

There were more dances, with Owen and Leslie and a few more of the young army boys. They all seemed very, very young to Samiel, who had been raised without the laughter they found so easy, even with their nation at war, even preparing to fight personally against elf warriors with centuries of experience.

He let Owen walk him out of the ball when the dance floor began to thin and the Gilmours gathered to go. Samiel was helped into the carriage and walked up to the Greely Towers. He was glad when the doorman hustled him inside out of the growing darkness.

Aileen and Clem wanted to know what he'd learned, of course, but he shook them off and commandeered the fire for some long-distance scrying.

Magelord Hartley's face was easy to find in the fires. He stared back at Samiel under dark, heavy brows.

"Anything useful?"

Samiel peeled the wig off and started removing jewelry as he spoke. "The humans have some sort of weapon that can destroy a city, or a forest, with only one blow. Or so a young human soldier of my acquaintance claims. He says they will use it on a forest, as an example, and then the human cities, to cut off our supplies, scare them out of the country." He paused. "Perhaps magical shielding, to protect the cities from the airships? Though he says magic is ineffective, I doubt they had anyone of your strength try." He wasn't sure how to accomplish something so large, but his father was a very powerful mage, surely he'd be able to help...

"Absolutely not," Hartley shook his head. "My energies must be spent combating dwarf attacks on our forces. The humans can fortify themselves, if they are concerned for their safety from the dwarves. I very much doubt your acquaintance is telling the truth; humans would not attack their own kind, and they cannot have a machine of such ability."

"I know a lie when I see it, Father, unless you forgot my particular suitability for this mission," Samiel frowned.

"Even you can be fooled," Hartley sniffed. "And you are impatient with the disguise already. You wish the mission to be over."

Samiel didn't answer, because that conversation was *never* worth having. His father would accuse him of shirking his duty and wishing to leave like his mother had. Why had he been told to come here, if not for learning the enemy's plans so his father could block them? If his reports were ignored, what was his purpose? He had done light espionage before, for his father, mostly checking to ensure the farmers were paying all they owed, not hiding any sources of income. But he'd never needed to cross dress for that. Of course he found the costume uncomfortable. His father would, too, if he had to wear a corset and wig in this blasted heat.

"Keep observing the human military boys. I wish to speak to Clem and Aileen. Keep the connection open. You are dismissed."

He left the room, sulking, but as he sprawled on the bed without a care for the fancy dress, he focused on not just letting Clem and Aileen, who had no magic, speak with his father. He did a quick bit of rune-work that let him listen in.

"The brat is as impertinent as his mother. By the time he returns, make sure he is…more subdued. I can't have an illegitimate halfbreed thinking he shall inherit the Magehold. He is of much more use as a spy than a son, but I should have left him mute."

"It is as my lord says," Clem said gravely. That was what shocked Samiel the most – he knew his father didn't much value him as a prospective heir. But Clem had seemed bad at acting and seemed to like Samiel well enough. The former was looking much less likely, which meant the latter was suspect as well.

"I don't suppose you'll attempt to incite panic in the human cities of elvendom," Hartley asked wryly.

"Of course not, my lord," Aileen answered. "You saved our lives, when Clem was on the run. We will never betray you."

"Good. Let the brat play dress-up for a few more days. Consider it a holiday for the pair of you. I knew he wouldn't learn anything I didn't already know. These 'bombs' as the humans call them might have all the power they say, but it will only incite our humans to fight back, outraged by the betrayal of their own species."

Samiel clenched his hands into fists and started rooting through his luggage, continuing to listen but hearing nothing else of value. He was careful not to end the connection until Aileen called through the door that they had finished. Why had his father said things like that, knowing there was a chance Samiel could hear? Was he so confident in his son's loyalty?

No, he just knew I couldn't do anything, even if I did leave. Metropolita authorities wouldn't believe a girl, especially not a half-elf one, and certainly not a half-elf boy they'd never met, or one who had pretended to be a woman. He found the boy's clothes that he'd brought in case he'd needed an emergency change of disguise. They were meant to be plain, simple fabrics: tan short pants, a white linen shirt, and lacing brown ankle boots over bare feet. He'd forgotten socks, typical. Well, better they think he couldn't afford them. He pocketed what coins he could dig out of the luggage and finally spared a thought to his escape.

He ended up just waiting until he thought he could wait no longer. Surely the Fagans were asleep? The silent skulking about in shadows, he was very, very practiced at. He slipped out the door and took the stairs to a service exit of the Greely Towers.

Perhaps Metropolita would not believe his warnings about the Magelord, or any information he offered. But the skills of a mage were in high demand, even here in this city of metal. He wouldn't starve, and more importantly he would never have to wear another thrice-blasted corset for an elf who thought he was a useful servant, not a son.

The Leprechaun's Story
J. L. Mulvihill

As an adult I never really believed in magic, until the day I had a strange encounter while running a steamship on the Mississippi River. I had been hauling cargo up and down the Mississippi all summer in sweltering heat. You can't get much more monotonous than that. The only company you have are your crew, which is sparse on a steamship, the alligators who lounge lazily on shore, an occasional snake, and mosquitoes that continuously buzz about whispering in your ear.

One early morning on a particularly blessed balmy September, the bell rang on deck for all hands. When I arrived on deck from my sleeping quarters I looked to see what the commotion could be. Out in the water, floating on a small makeshift raft, was a little man.

The first mate used the grappling hook once we got close enough to pull the raft closer to the ship. The little man seemed to be unconscious or dead since he could not be woken from his slumber. To my surprise the first mate then hooked the little man by the wide black belt strapped about the man's waist and lifted him aboard.

He laid him on the deck and we all got a look at the smallest human we had ever seen. Dressed in a little white shirt and little brown breeches, held up by tiny little suspenders, and ending in child-size boots he almost looked like a three-foot doll. He had reddish brown hair and a beard the same color that came down to his chest.

After we determined the man still lived, we took him below and Cooky, our cook, did what he could to revive him. He tried everything, but nothing worked until he poured some Tennessee whiskey down his throat.

You never saw someone revive so quickly in all your life. That little man shot up into a sitting position, eyes wide open like a scared little rabbit staring about. Then he reached for the bottle of whiskey in Cooky's hands and, quicker than you could spit, the little man grabbed that bottle and drank it down to nothing.

A smile spread across his face and he said in the thickest Irish accent I ever heard in America, "Well, don't that beat all, and me thinkin' you Americans couldn't match me *uisce beatha*, here ye go makin' somthin' like this. And what do you call this?" He asked as he sucked the last drop from the bottle.

Well it took all of us a moment to adjust to his accent before Cooky spoke up. "That was Jack Daniels, my private stash," Cooky said a little breathless and shocked.

"Oh, you looked to be of fine Irish descent my boy. It's not whiskey mind ya, but it'll do in a pinch and I thank ye for your sacrifice. I should be givin' ye the first wish then."

"First wish?" I asked. "What do you think you are, a Leprechaun?"

We all had a bit of a giggle for a moment until the little man's face took on such seriousness that we stopped laughing. Suddenly, I felt ashamed at our treatment of a near drowned soul who had not even time to tell his story.

"All of you but Rodger and Cooky get back to your duties," I commanded abruptly to cover my embarrassment. Everyone dispersed except Rodger, my first mate, Cooky, and myself I commenced with the introductions to the little man as I should have in the first place. "Sir, I am Captain Wallaby Smith, this is my First Mate, Rodger Brant, and Cooky, our cook. I apologize for our inconsideration and offer our assistance to you."

"Well that's more like it, laddie," he said with a smile. "So who fished me out of that wretched fish pond?" he asked.

"Rodger did," I answered.

"Well then Rodger you shall have the second wish, and Captain, since it is your ship, you shall have me third," he said.

"Well, Sir, that is mighty kind of you, but may we inquire as to your name and how you came to be in our mighty river?" I asked.

"I've been chasin' about in search of my friend Imish for centuries," he said.

"Imish? Where did he disappear from?" I asked ignoring his reference to centuries. It may have been possible, I thought, that this small man had been shipwrecked and floating about for days in the heat without anything but the muddy waters of the Mississippi to drink. He could very well have been delirious.

"Imish had a workshop back in Ballywillan. Aw, but I shouldn't be tellin' ya that now should I?" he said with a wink. Then he turned to Cooky and asked, "What would yer wish be now, Sir? Surely you bein' a darky here in these parts, you be wantin' yer freedom then?"

"I am a free man," Cooky huffed. "The only thing I want in my life that I don't got is to be a younger man with a family."

I looked at Cooky a moment, studying the old black man that stood next to me. His hair silver as the full moon and the lines that stretched across his face mapped out the years of his life. I had known Cooky a long time but I had never known he didn't have a family. I guess I had never asked. It saddened me that I had never taken the time to find out anything about Cooky. Where he came from and where he wanted to go. As a Captain, you just didn't talk much with your crew because there was always a new crew every year, except for Cooky. Cooky had been on this steamship long before me. He became very much part of the ship and like the paddles wheels that pressed the ship forward, I just assumed his presence. Cooky looked at me, then looked at the little man and just shook his head and walked away.

I looked at the little man who just smiled and tapped his index finger on the side of his nose twice, then sat back and asked, "Have you got any smoke, my good Sir?"

"Yes, in the wheelhouse. I'll fetch it, captain," said Rodger.

"Fine, Rodger," I said, "but I'll go with you. I need to make sure we are steady flow and haven't veered off our course. We will be back, Sir, to check on your convalescence before long," I said to the little man, and we left to go up deck.

"Captain?" asked Rodger. "Do you really think he is a Leprechaun?"

Rodger was born and bred in the south and was a good southern boy. I had been raised in Pennsylvania, but my family had hailed from the old country of Ireland. I had been raised on tales of fae folk and the like as a boy, but as a man I knew Leprechauns, Dwarves, Goblins, and Faeries were for kids. I had no time for such nonsense.

"No, Rodger," I said, "I think he is a very good actor. He probably makes his money defrauding poor souls. In fact, that's probably how he ended up in the middle of the river on that raft. We'll look after him until Port Vicksburg, and then send him on his way. Until then Rodger, you best be wary of the little man and warn the crew as well to watch their wallets."

"Aye, Sir," said Rodger and went to fetch the tobacco while I checked the ship's coordinates and speed. Rodger left me as I poured over our maps, so I returned to the bunk where we had put our visitor, hoping to see Rodger there. When I arrived at the bunk, the little man sat alone smoking his pipe and looking out through the porthole at the Delta as it passed us by.

"Where is Rodger?" I asked. "I thought he would be here entertaining you."

He looked over at me and smiled. "Oh, yer first mate just made his wish. He's a good lad and I suspect he'll give ya a run for yer money."

I thought on this a moment and realized that if Rodger had wished for anything it probably would have been his own ship to captain. I looked the little man over thinking could it be possible that he really is a Leprechaun.

"I'll be back," I stated, and went to look for Rodger.

Neither Rodger nor Cooky could be found anywhere aboard ship. After I had exhausted my search, I set the crew to find them, with no luck. I decided finally that either this little man was a murderer and caused my mates their death or to go overboard, or by some strangeness he really was a Leprechaun.

Returning to his bunk, I had decided to call his bluff. I knew from my childhood that when you catch a Leprechaun he is obligated to give you his pot of gold. This would be my wish and I would see how he managed to grant it.

"I see you have granted everyone's wish but mine, little man," I said. "When will I be getting my wish?"

"Oh you need only ask, Captain. I am obliged to give it to you, as you know," he said as jolly as a Christmas Elf.

"Okay, then, if you are really a Leprechaun then, by the rules, I have captured you and therefore you are obligated to give me your pot of gold," I said.

He started to laugh and then cough and it took him a while to gain his composure, but at last he quieted and looked me square in the eye. "Did I tell you yet how I came to be here on your river?" he asked me.

"No," I said, "but let's not get distracted by that, you owe me a pot of gold." I was fully aware of the stories from the old land, of how the Leprechauns distracted and cheated those folks who tried to abide by the rules of lore and collect their prize.

"We'll get back to yer gold in time, I'll tell ye first how I came to be on yer ship. I feel it's important for you to know me a bit don't you?" he said, smiling as he sat back in the berth.

"You see, Imish, you remember me mentioning Imish, he had been workin' for days in his shop," the little man said as he tapped his pipe. "You could hear all sort of noises comin' from behind them doors but no one bothered old Imish, we knew better. Once Imish got to workin' on somethin' there's no stoppin' him. So after about five'r six days, Imish comes out'a the workshop with his creation. You would not believe it," the little man shook his head. "It were not but a human shoe, oh, but I think it was more than human, and I says to Imish, 'Imish what've you got there?' and Imish says 'It's a steamship.' Very much like the likes of yours but it were made from a shoe." The little man laughed at me and his eyes twinkled with merriment. "Well it turns out that old Imish had gone up to Olympia's to get that there flying shoe from, who's that imp?" he scratched his chin a moment then, "Oh, yes, Hermes, I think. Anyway he went to steal a shoe from Hermes because he wanted to make a dirigible, but he couldn't find the flying shoes. He almost got caught I guess, and had to dash out. Well, I guess he didn't want to come back empty-handed, so he grabbed the first shoe he found, which turned out to be Tethys', the goddess of freshwater. So when he got back, he decided that makin' a steamboat would be the best to do with that shoe. Well, no finer steamship you'd ever seen, with a paddle wheel at the heel and the steering wheel set atop the laces. Believe it or not, he set the thing to water the very next day and na'y a word we've heard from him since."

The little man sat back and lit his pipe blowing perfect smoke rings that circled above him. I straightened my hat, crossed my arms over my chest, and stared the little man down. He had to be no taller than the top of my boot, so I had to assume that, if his story were true, a goddess' shoe must be larger than the human's.

"That's a fine story Leprechaun," I said to him, "but I'm a steamship captain. I don't know much about you little folk and your magic or even Greek gods and goddesses. Why don't you just tell me about that gold you owe me now that I've caught you?"

The little man smiled at me a knowing smile with that twinkle in his eye. "If that is your wish," he said and tapped the side of his nose with his index finger twice.

The Witch Of Midnight Hollow
Alexander S. Brown

It was November 1, 1811 when Detective Xavier Hess was forced to think beyond the logic of what his scientific mind and detective skills could comprehend. On this gloomy evening as he was becoming settled into bed with a brew of hot tea and a book, he was disturbed by a frantic series of bangs that rattled his front door and caused his heart to skip a beat.

Being a believer of the superstitious and paranormal, Hess would have been more startled of some haint or ghoul waiting upon his doorstep, instead of a victim who had escaped the clutches of something much more insidious. The stranger who wept on his doorstep this lonesome winter's night was none other than a thirteen year old child who appeared malnourished and shaken.

Once the boy was welcomed in from the bone chilling winds, Detective Hess was unsure if he should fetch a doctor or an undertaker, for the boy seemed he could improve or further decline. This speechless child that glared blankly was filthy from head to toe and reeked of what seemed to be lack of hygiene for the last month. The smell, if not the sight of this pitiful teenager, was enough to bring tears to Detective Hess' eyes.

Despite the fact the stranger was dirtier than a dog, Hess quickly stripped his bedding of his mother's quilt and wrapped the boy in its security, then brought him to the fireplace. Disconcerted as to why this vagrant was at his doorstep, Detective Hess felt it was best to improve the boy's health before he investigated the matter.

A remainder of stew was heated upon a wood burning stove for the stranger. As Hess prepared the leftovers, he had acknowledged the boy. His platinum blonde hair was highlighted in a dirty grime, and his skin was as white as milk. Splotched indirectly all over the adolescent were stained patches of old blood and dingy bruises.

This adolescent still shook as if the warmth of this cottage held no effect. In conclusion, Hess was indecisive to whether the boy was shaking out of fear or the freezing weather that he was rescued from. Perhaps his tremors were caused by a mixture of both, as the blank stare he portrayed depicted shock, although he was dressed in ill-fitting attire for this frigid weather.

The garments covering this youth were all shredded, almost leaving the boy nude if it had not been for few surviving stitches. The stained Edwardian shirt he wore exposed his slim belly and part of his back, one arm of the shirt was missing and the other was torn to flaps, just as his ripped black trousers. Worst of all, his feet were bare, cracked, bloody and slightly blue. At last, the boy spoke, "I got away."

As the stew heated, Xavier went to the boy and asked, "You got away from whom?"

"A witch."

The very word made Xavier's body tense. "Dear boy, you must be confused," he coaxed, hoping that the stranger was more imaginative than he was truthful. "What is your name?"

"Jasper Black," he answered with his voice guttural.

"You must be thirsty," Xavier notified, then rushed to a pitcher and poured a helping of room temperature water that had earlier been pumped from his cistern.

Xavier handed Jasper the refreshment and he drank heavily. Lines of clear liquid streamed down his dirty chin and highlighted the filth-painted face with lines of thinned mud.

"Where are your parents?" Detective Hess inquired as he refilled his cup with another helping of water.

"They are slaves."

"Slaves of whom?"

The boy ignored the question and gulped the water with such intensity that after the second helping was chugged, he coughed.

"There, there," Hess said, patting Jasper on his frail back.

The boy caught his breath and wiped the grimy water tracks from his chin with the back of his hand. "The witch has them."

"Who is this witch you speak of?"

"Tesfa Del Morte," the boy answered. His body shivered and stiffened as if her very name was a bad omen. "She came in early October, she did. All dressed in black and travelin' with nothin' more than a broom and a black beastly cat... First time I saw her, she gave me a fright. Her long black cloak flappin' in the wind, just like her gray hair, and that face all snarled and twisted like she was growlin' at the townsfolk."

"Did anyone approach her?"

"No, they were too afrightened…"

"Why would a witch come to- I'm sorry boy, where are you from?"

"Midnight Hollow."

"Yes, Midnight Hollow. Why would a witch come to Midnight Hollow?" Xavier asked, the name sounding peculiar to him and foreign all the same.

"Our town… It be a magical one, it is. Our Lord, Count Von Adonis, was a vampire king. Back when my great ancestors were young, a vampire terrorized our village and it was Count Adonis who was brave enough to slay the monster. But, before he could successfully kill the nosferatu, it had bitten him."

"If this is so, what prevented your village from slaying the Count?"

"You see, even though the Count had been bitten, he remained good at heart, as he was a pure soul. Many of our townsfolk believed he would protect us from darkness and he did for many a year. In gratitude we served him with fresh blood from our livestock."

Detective Hess was hesitant to trust Jasper. However, he attempted to keep an open mind as there had to be some reason for the child to appear on his doorstep. Even still, if this tale were figments of an imaginative nature, Hess decided he wouldn't blame Jasper. Sometimes, deep psychological trauma would cause a victim to create a fantasy world, allowing the sufferer an easier way to cope. "Then why did he allow the witch to enslave your town?"

"He didn't," the boy defended, "he was a powerful vampire, he was... With powers so great that magical folk all over the land came to his aid for assistance and he would assist them only if their heart were pure and were free from hate."

"The witch harbored hate, did she not?"

"Yes, sir, she did," the boy answered. His statement making Hess feel twenty years older than he actually was. "She came into town and went to Count Von Adonis, asking him to grant her eternal life, as she was too old and feeble to live on her magic alone."

"And he denied her?"

"Yes, sir, he did. And when he did, she slayed him and drank of his blood, gaining his power and eternal life. Since then, she has enslaved Midnight Hollow so that we serve her every need."

Xavier went to the stove and fetched the helping of stew and served Jasper while mulling the story over. The bowl wasn't hot to the touch but warm enough that Jasper could scarf down a hearty meal without scalding his mouth. As expected, the boy shoveled the offering down, seemingly at times that he had paused breathing in order to satisfy his hunger.

"How did you escape?" Hess asked.

"Today when she was sleeping, I pulled at my chains like how I always do. I had done this for many days and this caused my skin to become raw and bleed. It took me time, Sir, but by God's grace I was able to slip out."

"Why did you not free the others?"

"She keeps a key on her, she does, and it unlocks all their shackles, it will. I wanted to help them, Sir, but I was too afraid, for her punishment for those who escape is severe and long."

"And you say, she is both witch and vampire?"

"Indeed she is, and her power and wrath is of great fright... I come to you, Mr. Hess, because word about the land says you're the greatest inventor for miles. Help us kill the witch."

It was this plea that enticed Detective Xavier Hess and his assistant, Mr. Larson, to journey to the city limits of Midnight Hollow. This town that once had the population of four hundred villagers had decreased drastically in citizenship. Horrifically towering in the horizon, above the destroyed village, a great nightmare hid something unholy and ancient.

Xavier's mouth was cotton dry, hands sweaty and knees wobbly. He hoped he was skilled enough to beat this old crone, who was likely much more knowledgeable and powerful than himself. Although shaken, he was somewhat anxious to see who was more righteous – a magician or an inventor.

The men observed, sickened by the crumbled structures that once stood as houses. Littering about the road ahead was a series of petrified villagers, frozen and now food for the worms and scavenger birds that circled overhead. Mr. Larson, who had recently assisted in a previous investigation with Detective Hess, mumbled, "Are you sure this will work?"

No, Xavier wasn't sure. Despite his insecurity with his creations, he felt that if he didn't assist these entrapped civilians, all residents of Midnight Hollow would die. Then Tesfa would harvest from another civilization and another, until she enslaved the world. Due to this knowledge, Hess knew as well as Mr. Larson that their only hope was the weapons gripped in their hands. This invention that both men clung to was a creation constructed by Detective Hess known only as The Crucifixus.

Before seeking assistance, Hess had researched repellents for vampires and wicked witches to find that silver and blessed water had universal effects against anything unholy. Sadly, there was a chance that the weapon he had devised wouldn't kill Tesfa, but only stun her temporarily. During his research, he learned that damnations that were high in power were hard to defeat. In Tesfa's case, not only was she an elder witch with a poisoned heart but she had gorged herself on the great vampire king.

Looking down to his hands, he acknowledged his steam operated gun that would expel silver ammo. Upon impact, these silver bullets would explode and, with their combustion, a thimble portion of holy water would be released into the victim.

The guns that would discharge these slugs maintained a wooden handle and a long, slender barrel. At the rear of the gun, above the handle was a cast iron bulb filled with scalding water. Briefly following this bulb was a chamber that prevented the water from escaping and collected a helping of steam. Upon pulling the trigger, a portion of steam would be released into the shaft of The Crucifixus, causing pressure to build behind the bullet settled in the barrel's front end. Shortly after releasing the steam, the bullets would dislodge with prosperous results. The only real question was if Hess and Mr. Larson could be a match for the great and awful Tesfa Del Morte.

"Yes, I believe these won't fail us," at last answered Detective Hess.

Even with his thoughts that he and Mr. Larson would triumph, there wasn't a guarantee that everything would truly work to their favor. Looking to Mr. Larson, Hess could tell there was minor relief. However, Hess didn't mention that this may be the very spot where both men would meet their maker.

"Shall we pursue the witch?" Hess asked, his throat and mouth bone dry with his skin feeling waxy with anxious sweat.

Regretfully, Mr. Larson answered, "I suppose."

The duo emerged from the crooked, narrow road they had traveled. Entering the demolished village, Hess observed a mass of dead farmers, animals and homes that appeared to have been struck by lightning bolts or some greater power of nature.

Practically shaking in his boots, Hess felt that neither he nor Mr. Larson were experienced enough to face the supernatural. Until currently, he had investigated subjects that were more tangible of nature, such as missing persons and cold case murders.

Advancing cautiously into the village that laid beneath cold, smoky skies, a gust of wind blew and with it was a revolting smell of charred bodies and brimstone. Fiercely, there was something much more malicious that was carried upon the breeze. Both men froze in fear, identifying the smells of Hell's furnace and a witch's cackle that had rushed down from the distant castle upon the hill.

Although both desired to turn around and tread back home with their tails tucked to their homeland of Percy Flatts, their obligation weighed too heavily for them to dismiss the slaves to the old crone. Before they could begin forward, a cat of the blackest midnight prowled into the open and paused midway into their path.

Unamused or startled, it sat proudly like a statue, its eyes of emerald fire pierced into the souls of both detective and assistant. "Kill the damnable thing," Mr. Larson muttered.

Considering Detective Hess had never slain an animal before, and he didn't intend to as of now, he argued, "We need the bullets." This wasn't only an excuse but a fact.

"We have enough," Mr. Larson answered.

The cat then roared like a lion, causing the detective's toes to curl in his Brogan shoes and his hair to stand on end. Without second thought, Mr. Larson drew his gun and pulled the trigger. A helping of steam became impacted behind a singular bullet. Shortly, their defense dislodged from the barrel, striking the cat in the head.

Still, the feline sat. The bullet that was shot had left the little devil unharmed. "What in God's name?" Hess muttered.

"The evil beast has nine lives," Mr. Larson feared.

The thing arched its front half downward as if in attack mode for a rodent. Growling angrily, it was shot at again, this time by Detective Hess as Mr. Larson reloaded. To the horror of both men, the bullet that Hess had shot was also deflected from the crazed fur ball as if it was shielded by armor.

The witch's pet froze then expelled a line of fire from its mouth no differently than a dragon. It charged forward toward the men, yowling, hissing, screaming and roaring all at once while it remained expelling flame.

Time between feline and men was swift but it allowed Mr. Larson another shot at the dreaded thing as it leapt at his face, its fire singeing his left side-burn and heating his cheek. It landed behind the men and ran into the woods, however, before it could disappear Hess was able to obtain a final shot, where the fourth bullet also bounced from the pest.

The men stood in question, watching the forest where the little monster took refuge, wondering why it had retreated so easily. Had the damned thing been nothing more than a warning or were they not the only persons who had attempted to assassinate the foul critter?

"Are you okay?" Hess worried, his voice quaking.

"Indeed I am," Larson answered then stated, "God be my witness, I'm going to shoot the black off of that beast." This was grumbled as he rubbed a hand over the area of his face that once maintained a trimmed side-burn, until the feline had burnt it away. "I wonder if that cat is responsible for all of the burnt houses and bodies?"

There wasn't time to stand and debate of what caused the village to falter. Hess said, "Come," as he enticed Mr. Larson to abandon his spot. Before advancing too far from where they had battled the little fire breather, Mr. Larson bellowed to the forest, "I'll send you back to Hell if I ever see your likes again!"

"Shhh- the witch," noted Hess as he situated another bullet into the barrel.

"Forgive my ignorance," implored Mr. Larson, "I have a temper at times… and I hate cats."

Shrugging off the outburst, both continued the road to the castle with their guns reloaded and ready to fire at will. "Do you think the witch knows we're here?"

"If the cat got to her then I imagine she does."

"Have you ever met a witch before?" Hess inquired as they approached the hills base that led to the castle.

"Only the nice ones," admitted Mr. Larson.

Pausing in the shadow of the menacing fortress, both men looked up the hill with a crick in their neck. The structure appeared to have been made by stone that was charcoal black. Securing the windows was stained glass that was smeared of raspberry and tangerine. At last, its great threshold blocked the house of horrors with a wooden door that looked heavy enough that it would require a band of men to budge it.

Then, they noticed peaking curiously from a window in the right castle tower was an elder white-haired hag, her face rugged and stern. Standing in silence, Hess was almost certain that he heard a parade of cries and screams from the castle. In between the wails of agony, the heinous cackle of Tesfa Del Morte and the roar of her cat from Hell bellowed.

Instead of bravely traipsing uphill to the deathtrap that loomed over them like a plague-filled cloud of doom, the men began praying, "The Lord is my shepherd, I shall not want."

Looking to the sky, hoping to see some form of comforting omen, they were dismayed to notice the sky was without sign of white dove or rainbow but was invaded greatly with circling vultures. Telling themselves that the birds of prey would not be picking their bones, they ignored the scavengers and were soon facing the castle doors.

When their prayer concluded, Mr. Larson suggested he go first and Hess cover him. Before the detective could protest, Mr. Larson reasoned, "No, don't be too brave. I'm replaceable – but an inventor such as yourself is surely one of a kind."

Hess swallowed his modesty and bravery then allowed the heroic senior to budge the front door, which squeaked when it opened and appeared to glide inward easier than expected. To the men, an opaque world was introduced with screams of pain and moans of torment hovering in the shadows.

Gradually, the team mustered the courage to enter the castle of doom. No sooner had they set foot in the living quarters than the door behind them slammed shut, causing Hess to jump and his trigger finger to squeeze almost too tightly.

In the hauntingly black abyss, light was applied by a series of sconces lining the walls that suddenly ignited into flames. The scene before them was an appalling one that caused both men to stare wide eyed with their jaws dropped.

Presented in the flickering ambiance, people of both genders and of all ages were imprisoned to the stone walls. Detaining each villager was a chain so short in length that each slave was granted only a shred of freedom.

Half starved people wearing dirty rags appeared no differently than the first night Hess had met Jasper Black. The prisoners began screaming pleas of "Help!" and "Free us!"

"Where is she?" Hess yelled. His question was unanswered as he was a soft speaker, which in most times even as he would yell, his words would sometimes be unheard, just like now.

In a stronger, more masculine voice, Mr. Larson hollered, "Where is she?" His voice had successfully gained attention.

"Upstairs," an unidentified prisoner answered.

Hess acknowledged the stairs to his right, fearing they would have to travel confined, dark spaces in pursuit of the hag. This, of course, would diminish their chance of escape if fate wasn't to their favor.

Mr. Larson was the first to explore the stairwell with Hess following, his gun still covering his assistant. Upon entering the second level of the residence, the men were greeted by a darkened hall that maintained an eerie degree of luminosity to shine through two stained glass windows.

Instead of stupidly charging into the unknown, Hess and Mr. Larson allowed their eyes to adjust, then they ventured forward. Distantly, down the hall, the men heard a posse of angered mongrels barking furiously at a pest that dared to agitate them.

Not allowing curiosity to get the better of them, they didn't investigate as the entrance leading to the tower, where they had earlier seen the witch, was to their right. They accepted the turn and traveled up a spiral staircase that was both neglected of lit sconce or stained window.

Moving cautiously by sense only, the men did not stumble or mutter once. Due to their smooth actions and ability to maintain a calm breathing pattern, the witch hunters were met by a door that prevented them from entering the room.

"Ready?" Mr. Larson whispered.

"Yes," Detective Hess lied.

Mr. Larson threw open the door and standing at the room's window was the hag. Instead of turning to face the warriors, she remained gazing out at the land she had recently conquered. The men watched, neither daring to speak or advance toward the devil's concubine.

The old crone was dressed in a black, silk bustled dress that was covered in numerous witchy symbols made of cobalt blue embroidery thread. Beneath her sorcery wardrobe was a pair of perfectly shined vesper boots with leather uppers and heels, nine inch lace-up shafts and pointed toes. Crowning Tesfa's head, covering her balding scalp, was the triangular hat of power that was garnished with raven feathers, dead flowers and an assortment of skeletal remains from rats, frogs and birds.

Tesfa appeared to be no taller than five foot five and she seemed harmless, yet, when she glanced over her right shoulder, the men were able to detect the evil she embodied. Flashing toward them was a pale blue eye, the side of a crooked nose freckled with a black mole and her withered gray lips were pulled back into a malicious grin, exposing a mouth of rotted teeth and fangs.

Mr. Larson pulled the trigger on his Crucifixus and the bullet dislodged. Before Tesfa could be successfully shot, she evaporated into a green mist that quickly faded into clear air. Quickly, Mr. Larson reloaded. Hess conserved his ammo for a more beneficial time, for they couldn't waist bullets on mere air.

Suddenly, an invisible force yanked Mr. Larson into the room and slung him aside. Shortly following, the same pair of invisible hands grabbed Hess and slung him beside his partner. Before either man could fathom what had happened, the door behind them slammed shut. Mr. Larson aimed at the threshold then shot, his results being unsuccessful.

"Don't shoot until you see her," advised Hess as Mr. Larson loaded his next to last bullet.

Hess felt a hand coil around the right ankle of his Ferndale black striped trousers. He aimed the gun at his foot. Before the trigger could be pulled, the same invisible force that had slammed the door shut, picked up Hess and threw him into the wall, causing his back to collide with the structure and knocking the breath from his lungs.

A haunting cackle echoed in the room. Hess drew his gun and waved it in the air with intentions to fire as soon as he had the slightest notion that the witch was attempting physical contact. Hess's attention was drawn to Mr. Larson, as he was screaming for assistance.

At first, Hess didn't know why Mr. Larson was causing a ruckus, then he realized the witch, in her invisible grandness, had seized Mr. Larson by his long beard and was tugging him to the stained glass window. Although, Hess couldn't see the hag he aimed his Crucifixus a few inches from Mr. Larson's face and pulled the trigger.

The bullet dislodged, missing the intended spot and shooting through Mr. Larson's beard, missing both him and the witch. Fumbling with his gun and ammo, Hess had successfully loaded the next bullet, but had yet to aim and pull the trigger before the witch was able to seize him, lift him up and throw him toward the window.

Instead of flying through the stained glass as Hess had feared, he crashed into the wall left of the window. Attempting to collect himself, he realized he had squeezed The Crucifixus too hard, wasting the ammo that was loaded earlier.

In a gravelly yowl, the witch called out the beginning of a curse to her elder Gods to strike torment in her hunters. Sluggishly, Hess reached in the pocket for his Frock coat for the last bullet and loaded The Crucifixus. Before he could continue attack, Mr. Larson began grunting as an invisible foot stomped into his abdomen. Aiming the gun, Hess fired, his shot was semi-successful, as a spray of blood misted out from a gash caused by the bullet grazing the invisible hag.

At last, there was visibility to the old crone as a line of bright red trickled down what Hess suspected was the right side of her head. The room filled with a shrill cry, causing Hess to jitter. Although she was stunned and her chant was momentarily silenced, as soon as she regained strength Tesfa continued her prayer of blasphemy.

Overhead, a black cloud began to swirl. From this vortex blew great winds with bolts of lightning striking from the center, at times almost hitting Hess and Mr. Larson, who managed to roll free from being directly hit.

The room filled with the witch's cackle and with each lightning bolt Tesfa was highlighted in a silver lining. The men attempted to aim and shoot but their muscles constricted, rendering their limbs useless. Hypnotized by the swirling black mass that engulfed the ceiling, the men noticed where it began to develop depth in its madness.

Rambling furiously, Tesfa cried out to her God. Parting the vortex, two red hands with black claws entered their world and the tips of bull horns followed. Quickly, Mr. Larson found words and he cried out the spell that he had learned previously by saintly witch maidens. His words, like hers, were ancient and full of power.

The horns and lobster-red hands were sucked back into the vortex that now began swirling counterclockwise. Tesfa was at last reduced to being a mute. Preventing her from successfully achieving any other sinister goals, Hess lined his gun up with the streak of blood and shot. Successfully, the silver bullet entered Tesfa.

A bullet wound became visible at what was estimated to her bosom. This blow caused Tesfa to regain visibility, likely not because she wanted to but because the silver had defeated her power.

Without second thought, Mr. Larson fired his gun. The final bullet struck Tesfa in her cruel heart, knocking her from her feet. As soon as the evil woman landed on her back there came a miniature combustion within her, shortly followed by another minor pop, resulting in temporary paralysis.

"Are you well?" Mr. Larson huffed out.

"As well as expected," wheezed out Detective Hess, "Where did you learn that?"

"I told you," Mr. Larson answered, "I knew a few nice witches."

Once the men had the opportunity to rest, they staggered into a standing position with the knowledge they would have to be bedridden for the coming days. Dusting themselves from the recent battle, they limped to Tesfa and peered down.

The villainess' face was contorted in a snarl of frozen anger so that her fangs and rotted teeth appeared in full. In her hateful black eyes they could see her secretly brooding. If only she could speak or move, they would be afraid.

Hess recalled, as he gazed upon the paralyzed hag, that Jasper had noted she kept the key hidden upon her and sure enough, attached to her pointed hat, beyond the bones, raven feathers and dead plants was a silver skeleton key that would grant freedom to many. Wearily, they staggered from the room to release the slaves and fetch aid.

When the men reached the second level of the castle, they paused. The mongrels were still barking angrily in the nearing room. At last, Mr. Larson admitted that curiosity had gotten the better of him and he had to see what had caused the commotion. Detective Hess shared his wonder, therefore, the two of them walked silently to the doorway and gazed in.

Chained to the wall were three double headed hell hounds, all of which were spewing green saliva from their snarled lips and all with glaring red eyes. Pacing back and forth in front of them was the black beast, just out of attack's reach, deliberately antagonizing the dogs. This cat who had nine lives was about to lose its remaining few, as it had yet to notice the men.

Swiftly, Mr. Larson stomped over to the cat. It turned and froze with splayed ears with a hiss of warning. Mr. Larson drew his foot back and kicked the fur ball into the jaws of the center hell hound. Turning away, he grumbled as revenge was his, "I hate cats."

Within that very day all slaves were freed and they followed the heroes out of destruction and into Hess's hometown of Percy Flatts, where they were fed, nursed and would join the population. As soon as the new settlers were taken care of, Hess and Mr. Larson had crafted three more silver bullets and ventured to the castle with a mob of men. The three hell hounds were put to rest and Tesfa Del More was carried back to Percy Flatts, alert and paralyzed.

Once returning home, the men went to the town blacksmith, who had offered an iron safe that would hold the witch for all of eternity and deflect her spells. At last, Tesfa was carried to the woods in the iron safe and was buried far from town and respectful cemeteries.

Left alone without marker, Hess and his assistant sighed in relief, knowing they would never have to battle Tesfa Del Mort ever again. Although this witch was chastised from her magic, her legacy lived on. With the turn of the year, Hess had heard stories from villagers. They swore that while hunting, Tesfa had called to them, begging for release.

Somewhat reluctant to believe if their stories were fictional or not, he decided to return to the witch's burial. In the event of investigating their tall tales, he discovered truths to their stories. Tesfa had wanted life eternal and she had received that in dreadful abundance.

Standing above her grave, Hess listened carefully to hear the witch cackle a cry of insanity, she screamed out, "HESS!.... HESS!... IS THAT YOU HESS?... I'LL GET YA HESS, WHEN YA LEAST EXPECT IT! YA HEAR ME?"

Hess didn't antagonize Tesfa. There was no use in doing so as it would accomplish nothing. Most importantly, although this hag had caused much pain, he was good-hearted enough to let Tesfa reflect her evil deeds in solitude for the rest of eternity.

When The Heart Lies Open To Steam And Star
Anne E. Barringer

It was "the summons" which opened the door and allowed chaos to make its inappropriate house call. Trouble ignored etiquette and did not even bother to leave Gundin Greyhame a respectable calling card. Not that the *Päällikkö Kenraali* (or as the humans labeled him, head general) ever received calling cards. Gundin liked his privacy and the sign outside his workshop, a full twenty inches taller than his four foot, four inch body, clarified his thoughts regarding any kind of open cave policy. Massive rust-red metal letters glared out from the white-washed oak upon which they hung. "Do NOT enter. Violators WILL be used for forge fire."

Trouble apparently couldn't read Väliseppän, Trí Dé Dánian or even boring Human.

"What in the name of a misbegotten kraken's behind?" Gundin stared at the empty spot on his workbench as if his king's life depended on it, which in this case, it did. "Me own brother or no, I knew Faorond's summons portended something akin to food poisoning." Veins of purple popped up and spread across his balding forehead the way spilled wine filled up cobblestone cracks. His meaty fist slammed into the door frame and the thick wood cracked under one-hundred-and-eighty pounds of tempered muscle.

Behind Gundin, acrid, soot-black clouds billowed above hungry ire-red flames as they ate their way through a portion of the woods bordering the mountain range. However dramatic the picture painted by the depressed-gray ash which smeared itself across the landscape, Gundin had bigger problems than discord or even war. Normal circumstances might cause him to question his lack of concern since as *Päällikkö Kenraali* of Blackmont's elite warrior force, leading the D*rengr Sotori* and protecting his country took first priority. Nonetheless, the crisis at hand pushed every other thought out of his mind, and no matter how long and hard Gundin stared, he couldn't bring *it* into focus or will *it* back.

It simply was gone.

Gundin ignored the pain of the splintered wood impaling his flesh as he surveyed his forge. He seethed in anger, seeing the disarray of the tools he hung with precise care before stomping off to see his king. Instead, only a couple tools clung with precarious precision upon the crystal-studded granite walls, while the remainder sprawled about like puzzle pieces upon his stone workbench. The anvil he forged some seventy-five years ago remained the only piece unmoved as it waited in the corner for Gundin to resume his pounding ministrations. The empty space where the last piece of his obsession for the past seven months *should* have been waiting, the one thing needed to save his brother, gone - along with his assistant.

The anger building up inside him stoked up his vocal cords and he roared.

"Gilgamore-Salminan-Felspar! Where is it and where are you, you clockwork klutz of a tinkerer?"

"Who?"

Gundin spun around tearing his fist away from the door frame and stared, his mouth open and his right eyebrow raised almost to his receding hairline in disbelief. There stood Lady Endellion Swyn'anian, of the Trí Dé Dána, the newest and most fascinating pain in the rear to enter his existence.

She might pull off the prim and proper look with some, but there clung to her a gamine quality akin to the most powerful, yet invisible fire in his forge. Gundin stared up at her and tried to figure out how to get rid of her. *I want to blame this whole catastrophe on the chit.* Yet, in his brother's throne room before all chaos broke loose, he actually found himself interested in the paradox Lady Endellion presented. Her hair of garnet, copper and flame done up in some fancy loose bun thing and accentuated on either side of her elfin face with twin ringlet curls *seemed* ladylike. However, her most proper mini top hat, colored in the same shades of verdant green as her feminine travel outfit, perched upon her head at a most impertinent angle.

She tilted her head and Gundin could all but see the actual question marks form from the amber-green flecks within her amethyst eyes.

Enough. I don't have time for flights o'fancy or stupid rituals.

"Listen Dandelion, why are ye here gel? I told ye to wait. I said I'd get the gear housing and return to ye and the chaos above. Can't bloody well see what good the 'Mistress of Tea' is going to do in a situation like this. Besides, something wrong with yer eyes or is it just ye canna read the writing on the wall?"

She looked down at his very empty hands, arched an eyebrow and just before she turned, he noticed her lips move in a wry smirk. The Elvin wench flounced in a demur manner toward the empty spot on his workbench and set her unusual valise with the carved ebon handles upon it. Lady Endellion ignored him while she formed some intricate symbol above the catch.

"Why you persist in perverting my name and ignoring my questions 'tis an annoyance most unbecoming of a Väliseppän gentleman," she said.

Gundin rolled his eyes and snorted. The thought of anyone calling him a gentleman was laughable. However, she ignored his derision and continued with her infernal questions. "So if you please, who is this Gilgamore-Salminan-Felspar? Might he be of Näperrellän origin, perhaps? What they lack in stature, they usually make up for in syllables. "

"The Gnome is me own assistant and the only one other than *me-self* allowed in *here*." The chit removed a few things from her traveling case without so much as a nod of acknowledgment to his statement that she wasn't welcome. He pulled his beard in frustration and muttered. "And decent tinker or no, I'm gonna kick his behind back to the time *before* the ancestors stumbled upon this pile of rubble."

"I fear this does not bode well for our world and the Summit on the morrow. To begin to work together and end the discord between the races, well 'tis a most noble ideal. Of course it 'twill take some time for trust to truly develop and expand, which we expected. But this, this angering of the *VandA 'SouzAn*, our god born Trí Dé Dánian ancestors, could take our fragile hold on peace and doom us all to extinction. Since you apparently have not the gear-housing, we 'twill need some kind of plan. Therefore, I believe at times like these, there is no better time for tea."

Gundin almost choked. *Wait, what . . . tea? Is the crazy gel serious?*

Endellion turned and held in her hands a teapot of extraordinary workmanship - something which might have been ostentatious save for two reasons. First, the miniature castle of Montaboura gifted to the Elvin Empress by his brother years ago, had been crafted from *Constellion*, the stuff of stars. A masterpiece of fluid metal with a temperature gauge in the shape of a full moon, it looked alive. The second reason and how Gundin knew so much about it? He'd been the one to create it. Still there wasn't time for bloody tea!

"Are ye as daft as your bloody name? Flipping Faeries and their well-mannered traditions . . .

Woman, me brother, yer Empress and the humans' Overlord have all been kidnapped by the Djinn, and you're nattering on about bloody tea? Did ye forget we've only got three hours before your god born ancestors execute them all? We don't have time for tea, we have to . . ."

"So, you've already come up with a plan then? You happen mayhap, to have a spare gear-housing so the *VandA'SouzAn* Queen can sing and save the day?"

Gundin's bearded jaw fell open and he felt akin to a volcano ready to vent its lava-red fury. Not only had the wench interrupted his tirade, she bustled about the room using her magic to create a fire in the steam chamber below the pot and fill it with water; as if she had a right to do whatever in *his* workroom. Elegant grace, she all but danced around him. Another click opened her valise again and she picked out some stupid crushed leaf infusion and the matching cream pitcher and sugar bowl while she waited for the water to boil.

"Well no, ye Dandy-reared, pointed-eared freak o'nature. Did YE foresee the gear-housing would'na be here where I left it? Because if you did gel and didn't save me a useless trip..."

The teapot whistled and she moved forward to slide the lever to the steam chamber off.

"Sadly General Gundin, prescience 'tis not one of my better gifts or I can assure thee I would have spoken of it long before now." A frown creased her forehead and echoed upon her lips as she opened the drawbridge and added the tea to the filter chamber. "Yet empathy 'tis something I have an overabundance of and something 'tis not quite . . ."

She froze and Gundin swore the shadows moved. The miasmic smell of cavern mold co-mingled with the heady scents of mint, cardamom and cinnamon from the brewing tea.

"*Kargaşa* . . ." she hissed.

Before Gundin could reach for his battle axe, the shadows sifted and a sinister midnight-blue shape snapped Endellion's head back at the same time an oily black dagger threatened the vulnerable space under her chin.

"Back Dwarf, back. Slowly remove your weapon and kick it over to the wall." Gundin hesitated for the weapon had saved his and countless other lives many times over. "Shall I create a necklace of death for her? Being a Väliseppän you probably would enjoy it, no?" Gundin spat on the floor before he carefully lowered his axe and kicked it toward the wall.

"So now 'tis ever so much clearer indeed. The matter Gundin, 'tis worse than we thought, for when the Annord Dé Dána are involved 'tis never a good thing. Methinks I smell the reason for dissension, and the stench of things which should remain buried," she said.

"I want the housing Dwarf, and I want it now. Turn it over to me, and perhaps I will only cut her a little."

Gundin looked at the enemy so hard he knew if only he had the power of a basilisk, their worries would be over. But then again, he created things with his hands, not with magic.

"Look around ye fool, do ye see the gear-housing? Because if ye do, I'll bow to your 'superior' eyesight."

The dark elf nodded toward the back wall and responded. "The tinkerer pulled a fast one and remains ensconced within some hiding hole. Retrieve him and the gear-housing, and give it to me."

Gundin wanted to smack himself for stupidity in the worst way. Of course Gilgamore-Salminan-Felspar wouldn't have handed over something they'd worked on for so long. It was then he noticed something else missing and grinned inside. *Of course, Gilgamore-Salminan-Felspar ye old nimble-fingered genius.*

"Gundin, do not this thing, for this cretin wouldst destroy it and any chance we have to stop the slaughter." Gundin heard her vertebrae crack as her captor pulled her hair, bowing her neck further back. "So, your queen plays her hand and not slightly." Her voice remained calm but soft as the words had to escape from a rather restrained airway. "Did you procure the crystal or 'twas that left perchance to someone else?"

"So smart you are, for one of the pathetic Trí Dé Dána. Peace cannot be abided, no matter what you try. Chaos must continue or everything stagnates. It was so very easy to convince this one here," he said and nodded at Gundin, "to bottle both ends with some of the ancient starship's metal. Ah then, how eager your magical musicians pulled the crystal into the corresponding pin nubs - along with the *VandA 'SouzAn* queen's own spirit. Trapped forever she is, and once the gear-housing is destroyed, no one can make another in time to stop what's coming. Dwarves will blame Elves, and Humans will be more than willing to slaughter both sides. It will be glorious. Now get me the gear-housing. I'm losing patience old man."

Gundin tried to find a way to catch Endellion's attention but his height and the position of her neck, put him at a disadvantage. With an audible sigh, he walked back toward the hidden room and pulled the lever. Gears shifted without so much as a single groan, and the door opened to reveal his missing apprentice. Only two feet tall, the Näperrellän whose fearful eyes contained a certain secret glimmer of hope, had to look up to Gundin.

"Hand it over, me boy." He said.

The Gnome handed up the gear-housing. Gundin turned and walked toward the dark elf.

"Place it at my left foot and back away."

"I'll do it, but ye need to let the gel go," Gundin said.

"I'll give her some air, but she stays here until this is done."

The terrible possibility that none of them would be getting out of his workroom crossed his mind even as the dark elf released the gel from his stranglehold. Gundin bowed his head, winced and then looked at Endellion hoping for forgiveness. He almost gasped and gave everything away when she winked.

Three things happened simultaneously. Gundin placed the gear-housing as directed and dove for his axe. The dark blue boot of the enemy smashed the fragile gears and comb, crushing them into a pile of useless scrap. However, when Gundin came up at the ready, a most unusual turn of events occurred. He watched Endellion whirl to the side, barely escaping the kiss of the knife and she splashed the boiling hot contents of the tea kettle upon their enemy's face and arms. A howl of agony echoed about the workroom. Before Gundin had a chance to move, Endellion picked up the metallic gear-covered sugar bowl and smashed it against the dark Elf's temple resulting in the sickening sound of crunched bone and he went down.

Gundin watched in stunned silence as Endellion knelt beside the unconscious figure and with her own knife in hand, she slit the midnight blue spidermoth-silk around the head and ripped it down the side revealing sickly white skin. Her mouth all but disappeared while she completed her grim duty, as she made sure the covering couldn't be pieced back together in the unlikely event he recovered any time soon. It was the only way to keep him from following in the sunshine.

She looked at the sugar bowl and then to the angry lump. She held up the sugar bowl which sported a sizable dent and made a dismissive titching noise.

Gundin looked at her in disbelief and then at his assistant who walked toward them. "Del, he was gonna skin ye alive and yer worried about a sugar bowl?"

Her head slumped and her shoulders shook. Gundin, certain she cried as shock settled in for an extended visit, moved closer only to find not tears, but laughter.

"Oh dear me no, tis about my manners, or lack thereof. I do believe my mother would be most vexed with me."

"Yer daft now, aren't ye? I've stout ale I can give ye . . ."

Endellion raised her face toward Gundin and a mischievous look the likes of which he'd never seen before covered her entire elfin face.

"Well then what's the matter gel?" He asked.

"Because dear General, though I served our 'guest' tea, and though 'twas in a most unusual manner, I forgot proper etiquette when I failed to ask him if he wanted one lump or two."

Emotions unfamiliar and rusty fought to free themselves from his gruff interior and he almost choked on the foreign bubble of laughter that escaped.

* * *

Adventure, she thought with a sigh, *must certainly be life's true panacea.*

Lady Endellion Swyn'anian felt like the phoenix must feel when reigniting from the ashes of its previous life. Now, every sip of tea exploded with full flavor upon taste buds once tired and bored. Each intake of breath caused evocative scents to dance, renewing memories once hidden away for the sake of duty. Notes sang full of color, while every color could be touched. *Each feels as unique as the different bolts of cloth in a tailor's shop.*

"And yet," she mused out loud whilst she re-pinned her hair, "all hope mayhap be lost as the gear-housing is smashed beyond repair."

"Not so, Dandy-Del, not so," Gundin uncovered the parcel retrieved from the hiding place. "Gilgamore-Salminan-Felspar managed to hide the real one and only handed out the prototype."

Endellion forgot decorum. She ran over, bent down and kissed the Gnome on both cheeks. "GILGAMORE! Our brilliant, brilliant darling. I wondered why neither one of thee seemed dismayed when that cruel tool of chaos smashed our only way for the *VandA'SouzAn* Queen to sing her truth." She smiled with good-natured grace at Gundin's assistant as he blushed.

"However, I don't know what we canst do about distance," she said.

"What? What do you mean distance?" Gundin frowned up at her, creasing more lines upon his already well-weathered map of a face.

Endellion felt herself sink onto the cushioned bench, a pool of dismay. "Gundin, the *VandA'SouzAn* Defender only gave us three hours to get the gear-housing and bring it to him at the *Dúlra Beannaithe Fearann*." The general shrugged his shoulders. "Doest thee not comprehend? We have mayhap one left, and at least three needed to get there. 'Tis simply not enough time."

"Well wench, canna ye no use yer magic and transport us there?" Gundin held his hands, palms up, before him. "While I prefer to use that which the Smithgods have gifted me with and ha' no love o'magic, in this case I'm willing to make a sacrifice."

Endellion shook her head, sighed and rested her chin in her hands. "Though my kith and kin wouldst perhaps take my words from me, I needs must admit that magic cannot solve every problem. My magics are small compared to the powers granted to my Empress and practiced by others of the Court. Elementals and cantrips are all I hath ever needed, 'tis what makes me an exceptional fit as the 'Mistress of Tea and Ceremony,' much to my mother's delight."

"Well then yer right, we're as screwed as a tension spring wound so tight it explodes." Gundin leaned on his battle axe and bowed his head. The long fringe of his rusted salt-and-pepper hair mingled with his beard and hid his expression of sorrow from Endellion. However, her empathy let her feel his hopelessness and anger at not being able to save his own brother and king, let alone the others. She felt like a pincushion, pierced and heavy with hatpins.

"That's it!"

Endellion startled by the high-pitched voice of the Näperrellän, lost her balance and her face jerked out of her hands. Sitting upright, she turned toward Gilgamore and excitement buoyed her spirit from out of the depths of despair.

"The wings, Gundin the wings! I forgot to tell you that the last time you went away to hook up your steam engine and harp to the geothermal pipeline in the Summit's pavilion, I figured out how to adjust the timing gears."

The little Gnome bounced about from foot to foot, clasping his nut-brown hands in delight.

"Fly?" Endellion almost tasted the awe and excitement that crept across the muscles in her face. "You mean really fly, as in the air, like a bird soars?"

"Fly." His smiling face nodded in agreement.

Gilgamore skipped out of the main chamber and into another room. Endellion locked eyes with the general, while a smile of hope teased at the corners of her mouth.

"Don'na get yer hopes up Dandelion. Even if he has fixed it, we have a problem."

"Why, 'twill they not fly far and fast enough?"

He pulled upon his beard a couple times before responding. "No its more like I have as much business trying to fly with them as a bumblebee. Plus I'm not too fond of heights."

"And yet, they do manage to fly, bumblebees do. If they canst, we canst too," she replied.

Gilgamore returned with a chest he dragged on a metal cart. Del moved closer; anticipation made her want to open the lock herself. Gundin walked over to the chest and she watched as his fingers fiddled with cleverly disguised cogs and springs.

Gundin smelled of well cared for leather, Dwarven ale and a kind of metal musk. When the chest of cedar and the oiled metal of the wings blended with one another, a new memory scent triggered within her brain. From that moment on, for Endellion, adventure would always have that kind of co-mingled scent.

With careful precision Gundin lifted the wings out. They stood taller than his assistant and opened wider than the general's well-muscled frame. However, it was the combination of *Constellion*-shaped feathers, which sparkled like hundreds of tiny stars within their ancient starship metal housings and stole her breath. They looked the stuff whispered of in long lost lore, a combination of magic, dreams and mechanics.

It's Constellion, and whilst the Väliseppän are masters of metal and alloy, only one artist 'tis known for capturing his subjects with nature's fluidity. Couldst it be so? Couldst it be . . .

Endellion reached over, lifted the teapot, and the stamp winked down at her – G.G.G. She sat the teapot down and looked from the wings, to the teapot and back. Frozen, her lungs did not resume their job of breathing until tiny dots swam before her eyes and involuntary muscles overrode her amazement. Eyes wide, her bottom lip parted with a soft small drop.

"Why Gundin Greyhame, thou art a worldly treasure and with none the wiser. But will they truly fly, these wings of wonder?"

She reached out and with gentle grace, stroked a feather. Sparkles answered the sparks inside Endellion's spirit. *Oh to truly fly!*

"So ye fixed it then me boyo?" Gundin asked.

"Yes boss, adjusted the wing gearing. There was that 'issue' with timing . . . the wings now beat in unison."

Gundin pointed out the various mechanisms to her and explained how each one worked.

"The mechanism looks complex but it's really a simple design. The going barrel houses a straightforward torsion spring. The regulator attaches to the balance spring, allowing the operator to control the rate of the wing sweep. A weight hangs atop the mechanism attached to the winder and returns some of the flight motion to the main spring."

Del looked at the backpack-like harness and the handles which would allow one to change course and glide. "And that? What 'tis that switch for?"

"It's for emergencies only," Gilgamore interrupted, "if you are going to need extra power to land, pull it and enough power should release to get you safely to ground."

Outside, Endellion put the gear-housing inside her valise, and tied it with spidermoth-silk to the rings on her corset along with some spell casting materials in small silk packets. Then she held out her arms and shrugged into the wings Gundin held, and buckled herself in.

"I'm sorry you have to go alone gel, but I'll only weigh ye down. Now hold still while I wind ye up." Gundin wound the torsion spring tighter and tighter never noticing her cast the cantrip on the other end of the spidermoth-silk rope. It snaked around his waist, and knotted three times.

"Oh I wouldn't worry about flying alone." Endellion cast one of her elemental spells and feathers moved her gently up just as Gundin punched the button in.

"Why's that?"

Del laughed as the contraption took off, machine and magic working together. "Because thou art coming with me."

Gundin's scream of outrage made her laugh harder, as it echoed across azure-blue skies.

It didn't take long for them to cross the distance via air. Endellion soared, both in spirit and flight. She ignored Gundin who grabbed hold of her ankles and held on for his life.

The *Dúlra Beannaithe Fearann* known by most as The Godsholm, shone like a living jewel and Endellion could feel the energy resonate toward her from twenty miles away. A peaceful, tranquil place, its grounds remained sacrosanct; no blood could be shed and all the deities had their own temples and followers. The pavilion, a permanent structure built by the Humans to represent their offering toward a permanent peace, raised its roofed arms up toward the sky and reminded her of an abstract bird in flight. She almost forgot about Gundin until the first tremor reverberated through the wings, causing a momentary lack of movement on the left side. Nothing else happened until they got eleven miles from their goal, and then it began to shake and buck like a wild burro.

It took every ounce of energy Del had not to veer off course and if not for her bit of elemental magic acting like ballast, their mission might have ended with them just shy of their mark.

Gundin yanked on her leg and she tried to hear what he shouted but the winds blew fierce and wild blocking all sound. The ground did not look soft and inviting, it looked permanent and hard. He bellowed, pointed toward her side, and somehow the words made it through. "The switch gel, the switch! Pull the darn switch – do it NOW you pointy-eared . . ."

Of course! The emergency switch – it should provide enough energy to get them close enough without any harm.

Del tried the lever and at first there sang a little jolt of energy, reviving the wings so that they continued to flap and fly. Del sighed in relief as the contraption steadied itself. She estimated they were only six miles away. *How I love the Godsholm and the way it renews my spirit*, she thought.

Unfortunately, calm thoughts fled as everything failed at once.

No matter how much she toggled the lever, nothing further happened. The ground continued to rise up to meet them and trees began to batter Gundin with their outstretched arms. Gundin became one with her ankles, and Endellion feared the worst.

So close, we but only needed a few more moments . . .

She shook her fist and shouted her defiance to the sky. "I wilst not fail!" Fierce and proud, one hand ripped at the catch on her cleverly designed skirt and she whipped it off while holding on tight to the material. Endellion's father taught her to be prepared come what may, and though her mother would not approve, her legs remained, virtue intact, clad in trousers of the same shade of green.

A flick of her other hand sent her last elemental air spell toward the skirt which now billowed out like a giant balloon; so it happened that the two made it to the ground with all their respective pieces intact, if in a rather unconventional manner.

"Endellion Swyn'anian!" Her mother cried out in horrified shame, and collapsed.

"STOP THEM!" A cold voice, filled with hateful disdain, ordered. "Do you not see? They are here to continue to wage war upon you!"

Endellion brushed herself off and pointedly ignored the Annord Dé Dánan Queen. Instead, she unhitched her valise with Gundin still tied to it, and bowed her head in reverence to the *VandA 'SouzAn* Defender.

"Most reverend one. We have brought thee what 'twas requested, a way to talk to thy Queen. We believe should this work, the truth of the matter 'twill be most enlightening." She held the housing out and waited.

"They try only to trick you. You've smelled the stink of Väliseppän forging and Trí Dé Dánian magic upon your Queen's soul. They seek to . . ."

"SILENCE! DO YOU THINK WE KNOW NOT OUR OWN VOICE?" The *VandA 'SouzAn* Defender's words rang out like cannon shot. He gestured to Endellion.

"Rise and take our queen with care. Väliseppän, fit your pieces together and let us hear our voice sing."

Endellion reversed the cantrip and the spidermoth-silk rope fell from Gundin's waist as he took the housing from her. She took up the crystal cylinder, curtseyed to her Empress and walked over to Gundin and the magnificent harp he'd crafted.

Twelve feet long and six feet wide, the fluid metal workmanship captured the beauty of a giant fire-swan, preening its wings before flight. Strung neck to tail, fifty-six strings waited to be plucked by feathered finger-wings, controlled by the gears and housing Gundin installed. Steam engine power coupled the gear-housing on one end, and the geothermal steam gathered and held in a system of levers comprised of both magic and machine. Endellion handed over the cylinder like a mother with child. Gundin snapped it into place with a quiet click, opened the valve and the steam engine came alive. The pavilion filled with beautiful music as each crystal nub caressed by the comb, triggered gears and moved the feathers upon the strings. Ethereal notes wept through those assembled while the *VandA'SouzAn* listened to their queen's hymn.

"Ascend and thrive," the queen's voice evanesced, "let the new queen rise."

Anger filled the Defender, who forced the Annord Dé Dánan to her knees.

"Never shall our sister be free of the crystal and cannot ever return home. Since you love the shadows, be forever cursed by your own deeds. Chaos' skin will become true as midnight-blue sky, all your kind hated and hunted by those of the sun." The Queen screamed, echoing the voices of her people, as flesh and fabric melted into one skin before she and the *VandA'SouzAn* disappeared.

Endellion opened her valise and pulled out the ceremonial accoutrements. The Summit needed her touch right about now.

She smiled at Gundin's glare of disbelief. "What? 'Tis always a good time for tea."

Wax Seal
Mandi M. Lynch

In the dead of night, a large, black airship entered the airspace of Trilli Proper. With no noise except the whir of its propellers, it angled itself directly at the castle, where the royal family was sleeping. Stopping not at all, it dropped a single parcel, wrapped in brown butcher paper and tied with twine, which landed on front and center on the middle-most balcony. It didn't whimper.

The explosion was so large it rocked the citizens of Trilli completely out of their beds. Within moments, sentries mobilized and took to the streets. They pushed citizens back into their homes. The Trillian National Army grabbed their weapons, threw on clothes, and swarmed the castle.

"What happened?" Colonel Edwin Walker asked as he ran from his quarters to the front lawn. He was one of the few who hadn't bothered to change, and now stood in pajamas and combat boots. "Somebody give me a report, now! Where's King Fergus? Queen Isabell? Has anybody checked on them yet?"

"I don't know, Colonel. I'm just now arriving myself," one of the soldiers said.

"Out of my way, I'll check myself," he growled. "Secure the perimeter of the castle."

The Colonel took the stairs two at a time and climbed over piles of rubble when he couldn't. At one point he was blocked by a giant crystal chandelier. He tipped it over the hand railing and let it fall to the rubble below with a large crash. By the time the dust settled around the twisted pile of brass and glass the Colonel had already reached the King and Queen's suite; he ran in the bedroom without bothering to knock.

Inside their private quarters, the scene was even worse. Queen Isabell's limp body hung in the arms of the King, his four-year-old daughter Sofia leaned against them both. Even through the dirt and dust, Colonel Walker could see that they were all injured; the King's right arm twisted under his wife at an odd angle, and blood ran down the little girl's head.

"Colonel," the king mumbled weakly. "Please send for the doctor."

The Colonel's brain reeled. *A doctor? Modern medicine?* "Surely, sir, I should call the alchemist?"

The King's head snapped up. "The work of the devil! What has alchemy done for us? Nothing. My mother had a little cough. Dead. My sons – both of them – minor issues. That alchemist –"

"That alchemist was a quack, sir. I don't know how he got hired on here. He couldn't have managed to mix dirt and water to get mud without help. But the doctors – sir, surely that's a fancy that we don't need to indulge in. Reiley is much better than –"

"Enough from you. Get the doctor from the hospital. Or you, too, will rot in a cell."

* * *

Trilli City Hospital was a stark white building that smelled of an odd mix of antiseptic and bowel secretions. After the Queen and Princess were whisked from the castle, they had been brought here in a top of the line steam ambulance – new to the hospital, of course, since it had to serve the King and his courts – horse drawn carriages were clearly out of the question.

Because of the trauma, the royal family was separated into different rooms. The King paced from one to the other, his broken arm tied to his side with a splint. At Princess Sofia's bedside, he ran his large hand through her fine red hair or whispered her bedtime stories while he entwined his fingers with hers.

At his wife's side, however, he was quiet and solemn. There were several gashes in her head, and the doctors shaved off the queen's strawberry blonde tresses so they could tend to the wounds. They bandaged the rest of her as best they could, but enclosed her body in a negative pressure ventilator—the contraption featured a brass tube, six and a half feet long, with doors riveted and bolted closed around it, in case the medical staff had to reach inside, and a cap that had a tube of leather sticking out the center, matching the leather of the cushion inside. The Queen laid on this cushion, head stretched out through the leather tube, body unreachable for those not allowed to tinker with the doors.

The King, normally imposing in any situation, shrank when he walked into the room, and just stood there. The sight of his wife up to her neck in a metal tube was too much to bear.

Colonel Walker spent most of his time at the King's side, but he knew that if something didn't happen soon, drastic measures would have to be taken.

The hours ticked into days and nothing changed.

* * *

Violet and Rupert huddled together in the cold. Violet's velvet skirts clumped against her skin and she shivered in the open, wishing there was somewhere she could hide and stay out of the steady drizzle of rain left over from the evening storm. Rupert didn't fare any better, his worn clothes unable to stave off the chill of the wind. In a rare act of chivalry, he pulled off his long brown cape and draped it over his sister's shoulders before pulling his top hat down further on his head.

"Why did we have to meet out here, anyway? We're in the middle of nowhere. The Inn has been locked and abandoned for years."

"Will you hush, Rupert? This is supposed to be a secret meeting," Violet said. "You read the note just as I did. Meet here, say nothing. We can't very well have it in the middle of the castle reconstruction or town square, can we?"

"Who are we meeting, anyway?" Rupert shifted back and forth, trying to ease the chill. He reached for his pocket watch and then changed his mind. He couldn't read it in the dark, anyway.

"I don't know. The message just said wait here and don't tell anybody. You saw it as well as I did. So shut up while we wait, would ya?"

"You got a cigarette on you?"

"Roll your own. There's some life everlasting growing behind that big tree. It's better for you than the things you buy at the market place."

Rupert started to reply again, but the clomp of horse hooves across the broken cobblestones drew his attention back to the road and off his addiction. The wagon looked as derelict as the Inn, and the horses looked more like plow pullers than anything else. Rupert exchanged a worried look with his sister as the carriage door opened and a strange man stepped out.

The man said nothing, but nodded in the direction of the old Inn. Before he even reached the door, the wagon drove away. He held a ring full of keys, and selected the right one on the first try. The man unlocked the door and entered.

The other two followed silently and watched while the stranger locked the door again behind them and trotted up the stairs. Violet and Rupert took the stairs more carefully behind him, worried with every step that they'd fall through.

Once upstairs, he selected another key, walked to a room, unlocked its door, went in, and motioned for the others to follow. He shut the door behind Violet.

"Now, then, we can finally talk."

"Who are you?" demanded Rupert.

"Please," the man said, raising his hand. "This is a matter of the utmost urgency and importance and I need to know that I can trust you both." He turned and looked at the girl. "My, you're only a child still."

"I'm twenty. Hardly a child," Violet replied calmly.

"Yes, I suppose you're right," he said. "My uncle owned this Inn. Your grandmother, although very old even at the time, traveled with him from town to town, for they knew a faith healer was a good asset to have."

They exchanged a look out of the corners of their eyes, but let the man continue.

"I assume I have your discretion?" he asked.

"I'm here, am I not?" Violet asked.

"One can never be too cautious in these uncertain times. Please understand. I mean no disrespect to you or your… lineage." He paused.

"Sir, the Old Ways are outlawed," Violet said softly. Rupert let out a snort of discomfort.

"Do I have your discretion?"

She cast a long glance at Rupert before turning back to the man and nodded.

"My name is Edwin Walker. I have very important business that I need your help with. Your expertise is called for."

At the mention of his name, Violet raised an eyebrow. "You are…"

"Listen carefully," he interrupted. Time was of the essence and he didn't need a long dialogue about his position in the TNA. "The attackers knew what they were doing; Isa and Sofia are in bad shape. If the doctors fail to save…" he let his words trail off. Everybody knew the king had a nasty temper and nobody wanted to be the one to spark it.

"I can't just do some spell work and not know what's going on. Is there any way to get me into the hospital?" Violet asked.

"Barely. I've made arrangements for you to meet the night nurse and tour the hospital ward. If anybody asks, you're interested in medicine – at least as much of it as you can do in your gender – and you're touring the hospital to get a feel for it. Do you understand?"

They both nodded.

"Good. Nobody must know that you're there for them. Nobody must know that you've talked to me. Once you have the spell work done, we'll meet again," he said, standing. "The full moon is in two days. Meet me here before it rises fully. And be ready."

* * *

"My wife is not getting better," the King said. He continued pacing. The King walked so much in the last few days that he could see the trail in the wood floor where he'd been walking. "Why isn't my wife getting better?"

The doctor stood calmly next to the encapsulated queen. "Sir, this is very delicate. Look at this machine. There are dozens of moving parts of copper tubing, steel structure. Her Highness is safe in there, and we're doing everything we can to bring her around again to us."

"Everything looks suspiciously like sitting around and doing nothing. Let me make something abundantly clear," the King paused and lowered his voice. "If my wife dies, you and all of your staff will be in the dungeons treating mice for the rest of your life for treason against the court!"

"Sire, your Majesty, we are providing the utmost care. Please remember that this is medicine...not magic."

"Magic! If I wanted somebody to chant and burn things, I would have done so long ago. You are supposed to be the best that science has to offer. You and your machines are supposed to save lives. Look at the Queen...she is not alive; she is a tube of steel, still life in near death!" King Fergus's face had turned bright red and spittle dripped out the corners of his mouth. "And my daughter! She was awake when she was brought here. Why isn't she awake now?"

"She's had a traumatic injury, as have you, sir, if I may remind you. Her body needs rest and recovery. The Princess will be fine; this I promise you."

"You know...on second thought I wonder if I should have the guillotine sharpened."

* * *

Violet snipped the last of the yarrow and tucked it carefully in her basket. With the sacred herbs now in such short supply she didn't dare lose any of the precious plant. She sincerely hoped that the herbs in the field were potent enough. After her brief hospital visit, she was worried that her magic wasn't strong enough to bring them both back from the brink of death.

"Will you hurry?" Rupert's whisper hissed from just inside the tree line. "They'll be around soon."

"If you helped me, I'd be done by now," Violet replied, looking up at the sky anyway. There was usually an airship sent around to patrol over areas such as these, areas where the old ways could still be practiced, and neither Rupert or Violet had seen one yet tonight. "Do I have everything on my list?"

"I don't know, I think so," Rupert answered. "Get in from the clearing and we'll check everything, okay?"

She sighed and tromped back into the woods. "I hate hiding in the trees."

"So does everybody else. But with Big Brother floating overhead…"

"Yeah, yeah. Got your list?" Violet asked impatiently. Big Brother hovered overhead for half her life, and she was tired of talking about them.

Rupert reached into his inner vest pocket and pulled out a sheet of paper. "Your handwriting sucks. Think you could write better next time?"

"Oh, shut up. Why did you put the list away, anyhow? You knew we'd need it again."

"I didn't think we'd have to go over it out here. Can't we go back somewhere more... secluded?"

"We're the only ones who know the way into the forbidden forest. Nobody's going to just happen to be out here. Now that the fence is up and the guards are unimportant, we're pretty much assured that they aren't going to find us. Besides," Violet added with a hint of annoyance in her voice. "It's a mile from here to the safe house. We're much better off checking this quickly and making sure we have everything than we are running back out here and getting something that we forgot the first time around. Start from the bottom since that's the top of the basket."

He sighed and slouched his shoulders.

* * *

The rickety old wagon bumped and lurched along the cobblestone streets. Old stone gave way to the new, smoother brick which was laid recently in Trilli Proper. Violet was certain that a wheel would break at any moment.

The Colonel repeated his instructions on how to infiltrate the hospital. "The guards are still with the King. With the death of his wife just a few hours ago, he's been pushed too far over the edge. He's been given enough tranquilizers to kill a beast, but he's still kicking and screaming.

"Sofia took a turn for the worse late last night. Pus oozes from her skin and we are concerned. If she dies, the Kingdom dies with her," the Colonel informed them. "The King is beside himself. Even though we've already caught a break in the case, he won't care. If the Princess dies, it won't be one act of treason, it will be the King leading Trilli to an all-out war with a neighboring country. We can't have that… but, enough about the case, the more important thing is that we need to save the princess."

"With the Queen's untimely demise, you don't actually think we'll be able to get into the hospital, do you?"

"I have enough in place to cause a disturbance. When the clock chimes half after eleven, you two make your move, do you understand?"

Violet nodded. Rupert stayed still. The carriage pulled into a barn and stopped. "I take it we go from here on foot?"

"Absolutely. I'll have already been long back before you arrive," the Colonel confirmed. "Remember, though. If you are caught before you succeed, I will not save you."

"And if we do succeed?"

"Then you'll be heroes, and you will lead the return of both the Old Ways and the Alchemical front. May the speed of the Gods – whichever you choose – be with you."

* * *

Bang! The noise rocked the hospital, and several staff members and a good portion of the stationed army ran towards the damage. A mostly unused store room was up in smoke, and forgotten bandages now hung from the trees like streamers.

Violet took this to be her cue and snuck into a side door of the hospital, down a long sterile corridor and turned away from the commotion. Room 46 loomed to her left. She slipped in. Rupert walked so close behind that he almost stepped on the hem of her long skirts.

A guard was posted in the room. Rupert managed to subdue him before too much of a commotion was raised.

Violet tipped her bag out on the bedside table and tossed a package of candles to Rupert which he spread at the compass points around the room. She stood the statues of her gods up, poured the contents of a cheesecloth bag into a soapstone bag, and reached for her matches.

As the flame sputtered to life, she lit the first of the candles. "I call to the God of the East, to the water, to the gentle animals that reside there... Hail and Welcome to us..."

* * *

Outside the room, the fire was mostly out and police had arrived to the scene. Detective Grayson stood chest to chest with Colonel Walker. "If your army was so good, why did they allow a bomb go off?"

"I thought you had the people responsible in your control. We were dealing with the King. You were supposed to deal with the criminals." He wasn't sure how long he could hold the police off from a full out search of the hospital, but all he hoped was that he was buying Violet enough time.

* * *

"I call upon Bona Dea, Goddess of healing, to come to her people," Violet chanted as she lit the last candle. "I ask for your help, for your service, to save this child from the clutches of he who tries to take her away."

She put two drops of oil into the bowl of dry herbs, struck a match, and dropped that in. The herbs immediately roared to life, a tendril of smoke snaking out of the bowl and into the sky. She blew at them gently.

"Curatio, Bona Dea," she chanted three times, and then took a breath and softly blew at the tendril of smoke. It changed directions towards the girl and curled around her head to form a gray halo.

Violet reached for the goddess candle and held it over the girl. "Bring this girl back from beyond, save Sofia and return her to the land of the living."

The door burst open. Detective Grayson burst in with three other cops, two army privates at their heels. Colonel Walker followed, trying to hold back the King and stop the Detective at the same time. "What is the mean..."

Violet, unmoved by the commotion, dripped a single drop of wax onto Princess Sofia's forehead. "Bona Dea, cure this child."

The King wailed and threw himself at Violet, but fell short by a foot. As the drip of wax hardened, Sofia let out a cough. The King looked up from the floor at his daughter's bed.

A nurse waded through the crush of bodies and towards the child. When she arrived at the bedside, she skidded to a halt. "Sofia, Princess mine, can you hear me?"

The girl's eyes fluttered partially open. King Fergus pulled himself up and crawled to his daughter's bedside. "My daughter, my precious daughter…" he sobbed into her sheets.

"What is the meaning of all this?" A disheveled doctor stood at the doorway of the room and tried to cross to the princess's bedside. "I demand all of you leave this room!"

"No," King Fergus commanded. He stood. "Colonel, remove this man from this room and the nurse as well. We will make arrangements to move my daughter to the summer house as soon as we can." He turned to Violet. "The Old Ways have been far removed from us for a while now, but perhaps they shouldn't be. You shall accompany us to the castle. My wife is lost to us, but my daughter will recover. We and our Kingdom owe you many thanks."

Survival
S. P. Dorning

Kerlak winced as the pulse canon from the elven Rake Armor blasted his left arm. His own suit was an antique in comparison. He could feel the water from the damaged limb leaking into his suit. That wasn't good. If water was leaking into his suit it meant that one of the cooling lines had ruptured. That in turn meant that it was about to get really hot in here.

When war had erupted between Kerlak's people, the dwarves, and the elves, all of the dwarves had been sure of a quick victory. The stick-like elven people were fragile in body and relied on their magic to protect them. In the beginning it had been bloody, and it seemed like the steam-driven suits that were piloted by the stocky dwarves would indeed be the deciding factor. Magic was powerful, but it was limited by arcane runes and sigils, whereas the only thing limiting the dwarves was their own imagination.

Kerlak cursed as another pulse blast passed by his helmet close enough to blister the skin of his face through his visor. This elf was good. The war had raged on and eventually the march of the dwarves was brought up short. The elves had developed a new weapon. Taking their cue from the dwarves, the elves had designed their own suits. Only, the elven suits were powered by magic instead of steam. Kerlak was unsure how that worked, but he did know it was very effective on the battlefield.

When the Rake Suits had first appeared, the dwarves had thought they were demon spirits summoned by the elves to fight for them. It was Kerlak's own cousin that had managed to kill the first one. The body had been brought back to Hammerveil to be studied by the chief builders there. It hadn't taken them very long to realize that the suit was powered by magic. Apparently the elves had gems that could hold a magical charge. This was stored somewhere in the suit. The energy from that gem would then be transferred by means of sigils that were inscribed in the special bodysuit the elves wore beneath their armor. The armor itself was inscribed with wardings and spell symbols that would remain inert until the pilot triggered them with energy from the gem. The dwarves were unsure as to exactly how this was accomplished.

Another blast from the elf showered him with dirt and small rocks. The suit was getting hot now, and Kerlak was beginning to think he might be out-matched in this fight. With a hoarse battle-cry, Kerlak charged straight at the Rake suit. He fired a percussion shot from each of his gauntlets and released a jet of steam from the underside of the left one. As he did a warning light flashed inside his helm as the heat inside the suit increased another notch. Kerlak knew he couldn't do that again. It might kill his opponent, but it would more than likely roast him too. The Rake Pilot dodged aside at the last possible second, holes sprouting in the elven armor from Kerlak's percussion shots. As Kerlak twisted around, he stumbled and fell heavily to the ground, flat on his back.

Fear clawed its way into Kerlak's throat and perched there with the dryness that had been his companion for most of this campaign. Every dwarf knew that the elves were devil-spawns. Working their magic and speaking with the dead. Every dwarf knew that it was better to die on the battlefield, with honor, than to be taken as a prisoner and then seduced by the corruption of the elves. Kerlak glance at the 'boom switch' built into his armor. That was a last resort. If he triggered it, it would blow the steam pack that powered his own armor leaving a fair sized crater where his suit had been. Hopefully taking his enemy with it. He growled and attempted to swallow his fear, scrambling to get back to his feet before the elf gained the upper hand.

The piston that supplied extra power to the suit's right leg began to make a grinding noise, trying to seize up as he regained his footing. As Kerlak whirled around it almost caused him to collapse again. The Rake Suit lay face down in the dirt behind him, unmoving. Kerlak knew there were only two ways to disable an elven suit. You had to damage it beyond its ability to function, or sever its power supply. The trick was finding the power supply. Each suit's was hidden in a different area. Each suit was unique. Sneaky elves. Kerlak could tell the damage he had done to the Rake suit was not enough to stop it from functioning. He had done enough to disable the pulse blaster that was mounted in the gauntlets though. The sigils of magic inscribed on the gauntlet that glowed when powered by the magic gem were dark. His percussion shots had punched through the armor and into the fragile elven frame inside. Maybe the blood leaking from the holes had blocked the flow of magic. Kerlak was still wary as he reached down to turn the suit over.

Suddenly, the Rake Suit exploded into motion as Kerlak flipped it over onto its back. The metal-gauntleted fist of the elven pilot cannoned into the side of Kerlak's helmet. Flash bulbs of pain exploded in his eyesight as he stumbled backward. Two more times the sledgehammers rocked his helmet from side to side, each time forcing him back several steps. Kerlak could feel the armor getting heavier as the hydraulics ruptured and the coolant pumps began to fail under the onslaught. Kerlak looked up at the Rake Suit as it hovered above him. Had it gotten taller? No, he had fallen onto his back. A chuckle bubbled up from his lips as he realized why the elf had began fighting hand to hand. All of its weapon systems had been knocked out. All it had left was its fists! The chuckle grew into a laugh. As the laughter echoed out of his helm the Rake stopped its advance. It cocked its head sideways, confused.

"You are wondering what's so funny, elf?" Kerlak said through the faceplate. The Rake just stood staring. Waiting.

"Well, since you asked so nicely. I'll tell ya." Kerlak was pretty sure the elf couldn't really understand him. Most elves wouldn't stoop to learn dwarvish and he wasn't speaking common. "We two are out here fighting to kill each other and we never met each other before today. All we know is what the leaders tell us, and they say you're evil. I dunno. Maybe they're right. The thing is, you won't stop trying to kill me, and that leaves me with only one option. You put up a good fight, elf. But I still have weapons." As he finished speaking, he brought up one gauntleted fist and aimed its percussion shot at the Rake's helmet.

The gauntlet clanged loudly as he triggered the weapon. There was an explosion as the chamber ignited and tried to fire. To Kerlak it felt as if his forearm had been caught between the hammer and the anvil in his uncle's metal working shop. The weapon must have been damaged during the fight. Pain blinded him and everything went dark.

Warmth flooded through him as Kerlak swam back to consciousness. It was a good kind of warmth. It seemed to soothe the pain and ease the tensions of muscles. As he opened his eyes, he gasped in horror. The elf was using *magic* on him. Kerlak scrambled away from the elf.

The elf had stripped him out of his armor, and had discarded the Rake Suit as well. They sat there face to face, with nothing between them except the histories and traditions that had started the war to begin with. Just two soldiers from opposite sides. It was the first time Kerlak had seen a live elf face to face.

"You spoke…good words." The elf said in broken, heavily accented dwarvish. "We not angered at each other."

Kerlak's mouth dropped open. This elf was speaking dwarvish.

"How?" was all he could sputter to the elf.

"Scholar." The elf said motioning to himself. "Not soldier."

It was then that Kerlak noticed the magic gemstone lying beside the elf. It was cold and dark. The elf had used the last of it to heal him. Why? It made no sense.

"Because. To stop war, we need more yous." The elf coughed and the white bandage covering his chest suddenly grew a bright red flower that spread at an alarming rate.

"Cripes, Elf!" Kerlak exclaimed rushing back over to him. The elf sagged like a broken toy and leaned all of its slight weight upon Kerlak. It weighed no more than a dwarven child. Kerlak eased him back onto the ground. The elf's breathing had become ragged and another of the red flowers had joined the first on the plain white bandage. It was dying.

"Why?" Kerlak screamed at it. "Why did you save me, you stupid elf? Why?"

There was no reply. The light had gone out of the elf's clear green eyes. A sob welled up from the depth of Kerlak's soul. A sob that he had not known was there and was unaware that it was coming.

"I don't understand, you stupid elf," he muttered over and over again as he rocked back and forth in the fading light. Kerlak didn't know why the elf had saved him, but he knew he would be unable to fight another one without figuring it out.

He buried the elf under a plain mound of stones. Kerlak was unsure as to what their rites and burials called for, so he buried him in the tradition of the dwarves. He placed the Rake's helm on top to mark it. As he made his way out into the darkness of the night, confusion rode him like a demon. As he left the site of the battle, he never once looked back, and he didn't take a single bolt from his steam powered armor.

The Black Dress
Nick Valentino

Lucretia's footsteps pounded loudly through the forest just north of Ipswich, Massachusetts. Her assistant Gabriel huffed behind her with a specialized handgun that glowed with a faint green light in each hand. The thick brush made it difficult to maneuver through, but Lucretia lead the way, hacking and slicing the brush with two razor sharp, spring loaded blades protruding from the sleeves in her dress. Suddenly, she threw her feet in front of her, coming to a grinding halt.

"We'll never find him now, Lucretia," Gabriel said as he caught up.

Lucretia threw her arm up behind her without looking and covered Gabriel's mouth. "Quiet, Gabe," she whispered. "He's close. I know it."

She reached in the satchel around her shoulder and withdrew a small bottle which she promptly popped the cork and scattered the contents on the ground around her. A few seconds later, spots began to illuminate in a phosphorescent yellow.

"I knew it. He didn't get far," Lucretia said. "This way, keep going."

They ran about thirty more feet when the woods lighted up as if a bonfire was lit to their left.

Without warning, a ball of fire burst through the trees and flew right for them. Lucretia spun around and tackled Gabriel, forcing him to the ground. The fireball whirred over their heads and impacted with a tree just feet from them. The blaze stretched into the branches and instantly set the entire tree alight.

With a quick glance at the flaming tree, Gabe sat up on his knees, held both handguns aloft and fired consecutive shots in the direction of the fireball's origin. The target fled, leaving a traceable trail of snapping branches and noisy footfalls as he ran.

"Go, Gabe, go!" Lucretia yelled. "Don't kill him unless you have to."

Gabriel turned and faced Lucretia. "He just threw a fireball at us. I think I'll have to."

Gabriel charged ahead, ignoring the foliage in his way as he made up ground between himself and his prey. Lucretia took off to his right, trying to cut the man off from a different angle. In just a few seconds, she was much closer to catching him than Gabriel due to her custom made boots that contained heavy springs that pushed her gait twice that of a normal person.

She caught sight of the black-cloaked man's silhouette take refuge behind a large tree. She paused and crouched down for stealth. Gabriel closed in and caught up on the man from a different angle when Lucretia saw a pulsing light from where the mesmerist was hiding. He was going to catch Gabriel by surprise. Lucretia reached into the hidden pocket on the side of her dress and, without looking, extracted a palm-sized clock. She twisted a key on the top and threw it toward the top of the tree. The clock made a noticeable thud as it impacted with a branch and a second later it emitted a sharp twang as it shattered, sending dozens of razor sharp pieces of shrapnel in every direction. Tree limbs cracked and exploded.

Lucretia glanced at Gabriel as he neared the tree. Just before he arrived, the mesmerist spun around and fired a pulse at Lucretia, not Gabriel. It hit her with considerable force, flinging her off her feet. Before she hit the ground, the tree limbs from her exploding spring clock fell to the earth, slamming into the mesmerist with great force and stopping his spell mid-attack.

Lucretia slid in the dirt but quickly scrambled to her feet and charged the tree where the mesmerist had been hiding. Gabriel arrived first and held his hand up to slow Lucretia.

"Er, Lucretia. Hold on. You got him. You got him good."

"Is he alive?" Lucretia asked, slowing her run to a walk.

"Yes, well, I think he is."

Gabriel unsnapped a pouch on his belt and pulled out a silver cylinder. With a flip of his thumb, a flame ignited and popped up a hinged mirror which shot a beam of orange light on the branch-covered mesmerist.

"Yeah, he's alive, just knocked cold. I see him breathing," Gabriel announced. "He's a touch bloody though."

Lucretia leaned over the man, pushing brunette curls out of her face. "Ouch, a branch caught him in the head did it? Good, I didn't want to kill him. We have a lot of questions that need to be answered."

"And how are we going to get him back to the store?" Gabriel asked.

Lucretia looked up at her assistant. "I suppose we'll have to drag him back. He's too dangerous to revive here."

Gabriel groaned as he extracted a length of rope from around his waist. "I guess I'll fashion a stretcher, then."

**

Lucretia opened the door to the shop, checking over her shoulder to make sure no one was watching although she doubted anyone wanted to be seen would be on the streets of Ipswich at this late hour. The shop smelled like leather and old fabric, which always put a smile on Lucretia's face when she entered. Silhouettes of wooden dress frames filled the room. While being a seamstress was a passion of hers, Lucretia only used her store for extra money and as a front for her true business, which was hidden in back rooms of her building. Lucretia ran a secret business that catered to a very select group called Otherworldly Investigations. Her clients were almost always politicians, millionaires and high society types that became involved in occult secret societies and gotten in over their heads.

Completely soaked in his own sweat, Gabriel brought the still unconscious man inside. He went straight for an oddly placed book shelf in the back of the room where he pulled a translated copy of Doctor Ox halfway off the shelf. A series of noisy clanks rattled through the store as the bookshelf automatically slid back into the wall revealing a hidden room full of filing cabinets and bookshelves. In the center of the space were two large black desks covered in stacks of paper and odd clerical objects. Gabriel dragged the man past the desks where he opened a closet sized barred door and deposited him inside.

Gabriel patted his forehead with a handkerchief. "You know, if he's like the others, he won't remember anything about his bewitching."

"I know," Lucretia said. "But the others weren't this powerful. They couldn't throw fireballs. That tells me that he's been bewitched for some time and hopefully has some memory of Mister Spofford's nefarious activities."

"And what if he's still bewitched? What will stop him from waking and burning the building down?"

"That's a wonderful idea," a voice said from behind them.

Lucretia spun around to see the man they just locked up staggering to his feet. His eyes were solid black, making his gaze hard to resist.

"Don't look at his eyes, Gabe!"

Lucretia shielded her face with her hand and dashed to a wall mounted cabinet, but when she gripped the knob to open it the prisoner muttered a series of words that sounded like Latin. Without warning, a thin column of fire blasted through the air toward Lucretia. She threw herself toward the floor and the fire missed her by inches. The stench of scorched hair filled her nose. Gabriel hadn't heard her warning in time and looked into the man's eyes for a second too long, rendering him catatonic where he stood.

Lucretia jumped to her feet and hurriedly opened the cabinet. She extracted a liquid-filled glass vial with a series of brass teeth attached to the end and jammed it into a box shaped handgun. She spun around and, only taking a second to aim, pulled the trigger.

The glass vial shot out of the gun with a metallic clank and hit the man's arm, sending him to the ground with a yelp. Lucretia dropped the weapon and ran to Gabriel, grabbing his face with both her hands.

"Gabe! Speak to me. Are you okay?"

Gabriel blinked rapidly then winced. "What happened? Ack, I have such a headache all of a sudden."

"You were mesmerized. I shot him. I'm just so glad he didn't get control of you."

"Lucretia! After all that work, you shot him?"

"With the tranquilizer gun, silly man," Lucretia replied.

The prisoner squirmed on the floor of the holding cell, the teethed glass still protruding from his arm. Lucretia and Gabriel cautiously approached the bars.

Gabriel put his hands on his head as if to squeeze the headache out. "You, what's your name?" he asked, kicking the bars of the cell.

The prisoner slowly writhed and responded with an unintelligible word.

"Oh, that's nice," Gabriel said. "What did you shoot him with, a bear tranquilizer?"

Lucretia blushed. "I think it was horse tranquilizer. It was the first vial I grabbed."

Gabriel rolled his eyes.

"Give it a minute. Often the initial shock is the most mind bending. Can you get him some water?"

Gabriel huffed. "In the last few hours this man almost burned me alive twice and attempted to control my mind with black magic. I hardly think I owe him water."

"Please, Gabe. I just want to revive him enough to ask questions."

Gabriel snorted as he turned around to fetch a glass of water. Lucretia knelt next to the cell, reached through the bars and yanked the empty vial out of the man's arm. Grabbing the wound, he groaned and rolled over on his back.

"Can you hear me?" Lucretia asked.

The prisoner's face scrunched up and a string of drool slipped down his chin. His eyes were still solid black but seemed roll about wildly in his head. "Yeah, I can hear you... You... miserable woman... I ought to... really... burn and yes, something..."

Lucretia spoke slowly so the drugged man could understand her. "I need to know your name and what you were doing for Mister Spofford."

"You! Be respectful... woman! It's Reverend Spofford to... you. He is a great, um perfect, man. And he demands your love... respect."

Gabriel returned with the water. "This fellow is really cracked. Do you think it's all the drug's fault? Or is he just mad?"

The prisoner responded by spitting at Gabriel, but it ended up landing on his own shoe.

"Hm, yes. We always seem to find the psychopaths with class, don't we?" Gabriel said.

Lucretia took the water and offered it to the prisoner. "Please, have a sip of water. It will make you feel better. I just want to ask you some harmless questions."

The prisoner's eyes crossed. "You're anything but harmless. Reverend Spofford can make your scientific soul burn. There are things you just shouldn't question."

"Let's start simple, then," Lucretia said. "What is your name?"

While the initial blurring effects of the drug wore off, the prisoner's eyes blinked rapidly as he began to succumb to sleep. "I'm Nathan… Abner. A true believer."

"Good to meet you, Mister Abner," Lucretia said. "Why did Mister, I mean Reverend Spofford have you lurking about the town?"

Nathan giggled. "Lurking? I was surveying… for others."

"What others?" Gabriel asked.

Nathan looked up at Gabriel with watery black eyes. "Other true believers of course."

Lucretia scooted closer to the cell bars. "And what happens when you find other true believers?"

Nathan licked his lips with a dry smacking sound. "I know a divine incantation… that helps… awaken them."

"What kind of divine incantation?" Gabriel asked.

"As if I would give you the pleasure of even hearing it," Nathan said as he slid back on the cell floor.

"Please, Mister Abner. Try to focus," Lucretia pleaded.

"I'm so tired," Nathan said.

"I know, but I need you to tell me where Reverend Spofford is. Can you tell me his location? He's never at his home."

Nathan let out a sleepy laugh. "He's always home… You're just… not looking hard enough. But don't you dare try to find him. He will send your soul to burn."

With that Nathan's head slumped backward on the floor, knocked out from the tranquilizer. Gabriel took the opportunity to tip toe close to the bars. "Nice work. He'll be asleep until tomorrow evening. Does that mean we can call the police and be rid of him?"

Lucretia sighed. "Yes. In the morning, pay a visit to the sheriff and have him locked up."

Gabriel rubbed his hands together. "So I guess this means we wait for Spofford to show his face again and try to catch him in some kind of heinous magical act?"

Lucretia straightened her sleeves as she stood. "No, my dear Gabe, we're going to pay Mister Spofford a visit and I'm wearing the black dress."

***

The next evening, Gabriel paced nervously around the back room of Otherworldly

Investigations while Lucretia made a racket behind a decorated changing screen. He fiddled with his sideburns with one hand and continually checked his utility belt with the other, taking inventory of his defenses.

"Honestly, I don't even know how you put that thing on. It must weigh a hundred pounds," he said.

The sound of metal clanking together continued from behind the screen. "It's not so bad really. You get used to it. And I'm happy to take on the burden when it saves our hides so often," she said, cocking a gun as punctuation.

"Well, I'm glad our lovely prisoner was taken away without incident. Even after the bewitchment wore off he was quite the disturbed fellow."

Lucretia mumbled from behind the screen. "Mister Spofford is quite the manipulator. He can bend people's minds with or without magic. I do hope Mister Abner recovers his wits."

She emerged from the screen wearing a long black dress with an off white floral pattern embroidered down the sides. The impractical garment featured a high collar, long sleeves and a large bustle in the rear.

"You look wonderful," Gabriel said. "Perfect for a formal dance party… or an invasion."

Lucretia took a proud step forward, withdrawing a shortened shotgun from a concealed and camouflaged holster in the folds of her dress. Her second motion was jerking her left elbow forward which slung a machete blade from her dress sleeve.

"Ah, impressive," Gabriel said. "Is that new?"

Lucretia just smiled, took another step forward and snapped her arm to her side which retracted the blade. In the same motion, she made a little hop in the air. When she landed two viciously teethed brass spikes sprung from her shoes.

"Now you're just showing off," Gabriel joked.

"I do enjoy my gadgets and the dress is pretty much at full capacity now."

"Would you like a cup of tea before we go on our killing spree?" Gabriel asked.

"Don't be so dramatic. We're only going to kill one or two people tonight. A killing spree would require at least four victims. Coffee might be more appropriate," she teased.

"Hm, it sounds like coffee is the last thing you need."

The duo left the shop en route to Daniel Spofford's home which was an old farmhouse near Lakeman Beach. The five mile trek only took minutes by Lucretia's one of a kind steam driven carriage which cut the travel time significantly versus riding horses. Gabriel's and Lucretia's breath puffed in front of them as if they were imitating the single smoke stack on the back of the vehicle.

Upon arrival at Spofford's land, Lucretia slowed the vehicle so that it cruised without the rumble and clanking of the engine. "This is it," she said.

"The house looks like a church. He isn't a real reverend is he?" Gabriel asked.

Set on a small field, Spofford's home appeared to be modeled after a white country church. Even in the moonlight, the Ipswich River was visible behind it. The property contained other smaller buildings as well. What was once an ice house and a horse stable flanked the dirt, worn driveway.

Lucretia looked at him cross eyed. "He likes people to believe he is, but no."

"That makes him even creepier," Gabriel said.

Lucretia stopped the vehicle and hopped out. "I brought the tranquilizer gun, too. I hope that's all we have to use tonight."

Gabriel stepped out of the steam car behind her. "But what of your mass slaughter? That dress has to be able to kill twenty people."

Lucretia jabbed her assistant with a playful elbow. "Maybe we'll execute the slaughter when you get a black dress of your own."

As the two approached Spofford's home, Gabriel opened his mouth to rebut with another joke, but before he could get a word out something grabbed his leg. A flash of light shot up from the ground and suddenly Gabriel's feet lifted in the air in front of him. In an instant he was held up by an invisible force and one second later, it let him go sending him smacking the ground rear first.

Lucretia quickly sidestepped him, pulled an oddly shaped hand gun from her bustle and took a defensive position. "Gabe," she whispered harshly. "Are you alright?"

"Yes," he replied, quickly standing up rubbing his backside. "What happened? What the blazes was that?"

Lucretia sniffed the air. "Smell that? Sulfur and something sweet. It was a booby trap. Probably more for animals than humans."

Gabriel patted the dirt off his trousers. "If he's that paranoid, what else does he have in store?"

"I don't know but we shouldn't linger about outside to find out. Let's get inside and get this done."

"Are you sure this is legal? Breaking into a man's house and arresting him forcefully?"

"I have it on the governor's authority that our business with Mister Spofford will be authorized by the highest rank of government. The last thing the governor needs is a rogue magic user kidnapping people and inducting them in his cult. Sometimes it's nice to be above the law."

Lucretia took the lead and moved as quietly as she could from tree to tree until they were upon Spofford's house.

"And how do you plan on getting inside without Spofford knowing?" Gabriel asked.

Lucretia shot him a devilish look. She waved her hand and dashed off to the side door of the home. She knelt and pushed a hidden lever in her right glove. A round brass tube extended over her forefinger with a click. She took a moment to look over her shoulder and without delay, inserted the tube inside the lock on the door. Lucretia squinted and twisted her hand which made a series of thin metal arms extend from the tube. It turned effortlessly, grinding the lock from the inside. When the grinding sound stopped, Lucretia removed her finger from the lock and turned the door knob. The door swung open with a small, high-pitched whine. They couldn't see much more than an old iron stove, and a free standing cupboard.

"Don't go in yet," Lucretia whispered.

Gabriel looked at her with wide eyes. "Trust me, I wasn't going to."

Pulling a double-tubed vial from her boot, Lucretia snapped the tapered glass ends off with her fingers and gently tossed it inside the house. When the gas in the tubes mixed, they formed a light gray fog that filled the room. She pulled Gabriel close to her. "Hopefully that will protect us from any spells when we enter. Walk behind me and walk with soft steps. Spofford is a purist when it comes to magic. He probably won't have any conventional traps or alarms."

The duo crept into the dark house. The kitchen seemed plain enough with only unremarkable essentials. The next room was a study and again only contained a book shelf with sparse volumes, a reading desk and a large white candle.

Gabriel patted Lucretia on the shoulder and pointed to his right where a dim flicker of light blinked from another room. Lucretia withdrew her tranquilizer gun from her bustle and headed toward the light. Mid-hallway, she stepped on a loose board in the floor; the sound seemed to echo throughout the entire house. Lucretia's face crumpled up in disappointment. She was sure that they would be discovered.

Waving Gabriel forward, they tip-toed past a small second bedroom and further down the hall. As they approached the entrance to the room with the flickering light, Lucretia pressed her back against the wall with her tranquilizer gun held up at the ready. She slowly peered around the door frame.

The first thing she noticed was the oil paintings of distinguished yet odd looking men on the walls. This room was much larger than the others and contained much more furniture than others in the house. Awash in an orange glow from a mass of candles on a small table next to a plush leather chair with its back to her, the room was oddly warm. It took a second for her eyes to adjust to the odd lighting but when they focused, she noticed the back of a man's head in the chair which made her heart skip a beat. Whoever she was looking at was elderly with wisps of unkempt gray hair sticking up above his head.

Lucretia took a quick moment to glance back at Gabriel. The confusion in her eyes made Gabriel worry but again he followed her lead. Lucretia swept into the room and in a few wide steps, she circled the chair and was upon the old man. Startled, he jumped from his seat, dropping a thick black covered book as he stood.

Lucretia pointed her weapon at his chest which frightened him more and made him stumble backwards into a small desk opposite his chair.

"Are you Daniel Spofford?" Gabriel shouted as he took position with his glowing handgun next to Lucretia.

"You've seen Daniel Spofford before Gabe, you know that isn't him," Lucretia said.

"Well, maybe he's… um, wearing a disguise."

Lucretia bit her lip to keep a giggle at bay.

"What's your name, Sir?" Lucretia asked.

The old man looked desperate. His eyes were abnormally wide, and his pupils were fully dilated.

Lucretia felt bad for scaring the man when she noticed his hands were shaking violently.

"I'm Wallace… Wallace Spofford. I'm Daniel's father."

"Where is your son?" Gabriel asked.

Wallace shot him an angry look. "He's away on business. Why are you looking for him? He's a good boy. He's done nothing wrong."

"I'm afraid your son's done a lot of bad things, Mister Spofford. We're here to ask him a few questions," Lucretia said.

Wallace turned his angry eyes toward Lucretia. "Bad things? You mean like breaking into an old man's home? Like interrupting an elder with guns pointed at him while he reads a book? Those kind of bad things?"

"We're sorry for the intrusion, Mister Spofford, but we're here on government authority to question your son," Gabriel said.

"Government authority?" Wallace questioned. "And who is the bean-brained government authority that authorized this?"

Gabriel lowered his gun. "The Gov-"

"Hush Gabe!" Lucretia interrupted. "We have the support of the Salem and Ipswich authorities."

"The Governor, eh?" Wallace said. "I'll have to travel to his office tomorrow and ask him about his illegal and immoral methods of law. And what does he want with my son anyway? Is the Governor afraid of a little religion? You know Daniel is a reverend now right? So our barely one hundred year old government is hunting down reverends? It sounds like the British are back in control. You all should be ashamed of yourselves!"

Lucretia began to feel like she and Gabe had possibly put themselves in legal peril. Sure, they would be absolved of their actions by the Governor, but negative press and word of mouth would affect the business and reputation of Otherworldly Investigations. She lowered her gun and prepared to make an apologetic exit speech.

Gabriel sidled next to Lucretia and just as she was going to attempt to calm Wallace Spofford down, Gabriel nudged her hard in the corset with his elbow. Focusing on choosing her words carefully, she ignored him and flashed Mister Spofford an obviously fake smile. With pursed lips and cross eyes, Gabriel looked at her as if he was offended, cleared his throat and jabbed her even harder with his elbow.

"Gabe!" Lucretia snapped. "This is not the time! What could possibly be..."

She noticed Gabriel motioning toward the floor where Wallace Spofford's black book was lying spine up. The words, *The Lemegeton*, seemed to pop off the black leather in faded gold letters. Lucretia was shocked. Why would Reverend Daniel Spofford's elderly father be reading an old grimoire on demonology?

"Excuse me, Mister Spofford," Lucretia said slowly. "May I ask what you're reading tonight?"

"I'm reading the farmer's almanac you ridiculous woman! I think you've intruded enough on-"

He stopped mid-sentence when he realized Lucretia and Gabriel caught him in a lie.

"Ah," Spofford continued. "Well, it seems I've been a bit sloppy in my presentation."

Spofford took two steps back until he was pressed against his desk and shouted, "*Ostendo sum verus ego quod exuro in meus to order!*"

In the blink of an eye, the elderly Wallace Spofford was gone and replaced by a chestnut red headed Daniel Spofford as Lucretia and Gabriel recognized him. Before they could level their weapons and arrest him, a thick rope of fire whipped around Spofford and darted through the air like a flaming dragon.

The fire impacted with Gabriel first, knocking him backwards and catching his vest on fire. As if they had a mind of their own, the flames turned and streaked toward Lucretia. With nowhere else to flee, she dove behind the leather couch a bare second before the spell stuck her. The couch fully ignited, sending a wave of heat throughout the room. With her tranquilizer gun drawn, Lucretia popped up from behind the flaming couch and fired the shot in Spofford's last position. She cursed when she heard the glass vial break against the wall. She quickly scanned the room but didn't see her target until he said, "*Frendo quod Effrego*" and clinched his palm into a fist.

As if two invisible super human hands pressed it together, Lucretia's gun imploded, forcing her to drop it and shield her face.

"You've meddled too much, Lucretia Brown!" Spofford yelled. "You have no right interfering with the natural progress of man with your machines and science!"

Lucretia remained silent. When she saw Gabriel rolling around on the floor not far from her extinguishing the last embers on his vest, she hopped up on her knees and began pulling small hidden levers all over her dress. The garment clicked and snapped as, one by one, plates of armor tore through the dress until her collar, her sleeves and the bottom bell were covered in an armadillo-like shell.

In one leap from her spring loaded boots, she jumped over the couch and barreled toward Spofford like a cannon ball. She screamed like a mad woman and with only a few long strides, collided with her target, slamming him onto the floor.

He opened his mouth to utter another spell but the words failed him as Lucretia knocked the breath out of him with her tackle.

She reached behind her, frantically searching in her bustle compartment for a weapon. Grabbing the first thing she touched, Lucretia looked at the object in her hand. It was another glass vial for the tranquilizer gun.

Disappointed with her choice, she knew she wouldn't have time to find another weapon before Spofford regained some of his strength, so she twirled the vial in her fingers until the brass teeth faced downward and quickly jabbed it in Spofford's shoulder.

The vial drained into her prey and he attempted a last second spasm to pull it out but it was too late.

Spofford twitched violently until the sedative hit his artery and his body involuntarily relaxed.

Lucretia jumped off him and ran to Gabriel who was no longer on fire and sitting up checking himself. His vest had burn marks like blackened Swiss cheese but he reluctantly signaled that he was mostly unscathed. When Spofford totally passed out, the flames engulfing the couch died out as well.

Once they collected themselves and calmed down from the adrenalin rush, Lucretia and Gabriel bound his hands and dragged Daniel Spofford from his house.

***

The next morning a knock came at the shop door.

"Wonderful to see you, Governor Rice!" Lucretia exclaimed as she waved her hand to welcome her guest in.

Governor Rice, accompanied by two men with heavy sideburns, strode inside the shop after kissing Lucretia's hand.

"So, Mister Spofford is in your cell?" Governor Rice asked.

"He is," Lucretia answered. "He put up quite the fight."

"And where is your assistant? Gabriel Constance is his name, correct? I want to thank him as well."

"He had a difficult night but I assure you he's quite fine. I gave him the day off," Lucretia explained.

"Ah, quite understandable. Well, I'll get to the chase. What will happen is Mister Spofford will be taken to an asylum where he should remain quite harmless. For legal reasons we've assigned you an attorney where a lawsuit will be placed against Mister Spofford."

"A lawsuit?" Lucretia asked.

"Yes, this will give us the right to put him away without the chance of release. We have doctors lined up ready to receive him immediately. You've done quite the service for your community, Miss Brown."

Lucretia blushed. "Thank you, Governor."

"In these times of enlightenment, there are many people that seek to use magic for power and domination. It's thanks to those such as yourself that these transgressors are kept at bay. Today, science won an important battle. For that, Massachusetts is in your debt."

With those words, Governor Rice's men collected Daniel Spofford and took him away.

Words in Eden
Lewis Sanders

Certainly no angel
on bended knees,
I confess
my sins
to gods of
onyx and iron.
But
words are wasted
in the Fires of Eden.
Dragons compose
haiku here
of blood and the moon.
Somewhere
a meadowhawk
is screaming death
on the lighter
side of dark,
And a paladin
of shadows
awaits midnight dreamers,
Spectral spirits swimming
in rivers
of crimson spice,
the wine
of immortality
vampires drink.

Time
Windsong Levitch

We Elves are children of nature, and thus not
Inclined to concern ourselves with the need
to control or manipulate time.

Sunrise and sunset will come and go, regardless
of what we do. Spring and summer, autumn and
winter,
will come when their time is due.

We Elves are earthly children, yet the heavens are
our clock.
And nature is our timepiece, take a moment and
give it
a thought.

One can lose all sense of time when listening to a
river running
freely in its own time. Watching a leaf falling from
a tree
to ground can be an eternity, I have found.

Then in the blink of an eye, I saw a raindrop go
racing by.

As for a snowflake, what can I say – one can watch
it float
from here to there taking all day, and never make a
sound.
I find that quite profound.

Now as for the Dwarves, no insult intended, for
some of them
I have befriended. But truthfully I could take them
or leave them.
Truly Goddess bless them and keep them, as far
away from us
As is possible!

This also goes for their infernal and oh-so-precious
Time machine!
For I cannot stand its constant spewing of steam!
Gears spinning
And grinding, pistons pumping and thumping!

All for the sake of their precious time, so at the
precise hour, from the
tip of its tower a whistle will scream so shrill and
obscene that even
a Banshee would shrink away in fear!

And if you ask them, why they need such a
machine, they would look
At you as if you had lost your mind! Then say,
'Why, we need it to tell
Us the time! It tells us when to sleep or rise, to work
or play and
Even when to eat!'

Time

Oh Goddess bless them! They have lost their minds!
Second by second, minute by minute, hour by hour,
day by day!
They spend their time watching their lives tick
away!

But this is just one side of the coin's argument. It
matters not how
either's time is spent. For when time is up, it's up
end of argument!

Adventure: A Series of Steampunk Haiku
Michael Greenway

Tin, Copper, and Bronze
Upon this anvil they take shape
Gears and boilers be

Hissing steam doth tell
Of foundry days and much toil
Birth to the machines

Iron gears are cast
Big and small shall they clatter
Until their time's end

Adventure lies ahead
To the zeppelin my good souls
The Air Kraken waits

Cast off the moorings
The airship creaks to a rise
With sputtering fiest

Gallant are we souls
Eccentric in our nature

Michael Greenway

Brassy in our hearts

The professor speaks
He's reassembled a man
A man called Otto

Twirling gear sprockets
Gnash in Otto's shapened skull
He's more machine now

Goggles black as coal
Hide the eyes of rattled mind
A heart gently ticks

Tin, Copper, and Bronze
Upon this anvil they take shape
A man they shall be

About the Authors

Jackie Gamber

Jackie writes award-winning fantasy, science fiction, horror, and various blends of the genres from flash to novel-length. Her work has appeared in venues such as Orson Scott Card's *Intergalactic Medicine Show*, *Shroud*, *Necrotic Tissue*, and *Rosebud Magazine*. Upcoming publications include a short story in "Dead Souls" through Post Mortem Press. Book One of her Leland Dragon Series (*Redheart*) is available through Seventh Star Press, with Book Two (*Sela*) slated for late 2011.

Robert J. Krog

A native of Memphis, TN., he is a devout Catholic and a member of the Knights of Columbus. He has been an assistant arborist, a bag boy, a waiter, an order-out delivery guy, a legal runner, a substitute teacher, and a History teacher, all in Memphis. He has several degrees, mostly in History, but isn't putting them to good use, though he loves History and can still translate Middle Egyptian, if he works at it. Currently, he works in chemical yard care and writes as much as a full-time job, the church, and family life allow. His published works include *The Stone Maiden and*

213

Other Tales (2010), *Babies' Breath* (2011, parABnormal Digest), several short stories on his website, and the novella *A Bag Full of Eyes,* (January 2012 from Sam's Dot Publishing). He continues to write and is working on finishing several novels.

Angelia Sparrow

Angelia is a truck driver who spends her off-hours writing. She has eight novels to her credit with the ninth, *Power in the Blood*, coming out in January 2012.

Kathryn Sullivan

Kathryn Sullivan is the author of the award-winning young adult fantasies *The Crystal Throne*, *Agents & Adepts*, and *Talking to Trees.* Her children's picture book, *Michael & the Elf*, will soon be reprinted by Guardian Angel Publishing and she has an essay, "The Fanzine Factor", in the Hugo nominated *Chicks Dig Time Lords*. Kathryn lives in Winona, Minnesota, where the river bluffs double as cliffsides on alien planets or the deep mysterious forests in a magical world. Any birdlike beings in her books only slightly resemble her cockatoo owner. She is currently working on a YA story set on a colony planet.

M. R. Williamson

I send greetings to you from Horn Lake, Mississippi. Being a writer/novelist almost half my life, I've discovered that my greatest love is the short story. "Quest for the Dragon's Scale" was a short story project that was done for *Clockwork Spells* trade book. Others include "The Cowcumber Tree" for Kerlak's *WTF Mysteries Anthology*, "Hell's Gates" and "Doppelganger" for Jennifer Mulvihill and Alexander Brown's *Southern Haunts Anthology*, "Spotter" for *Flesh and Blood*, "Caroline's Wings" for *Memphis Magazine*, "The Timebender" for *Apex*, "The Obsidian Orb" for *Clark's World*, "The Hide-A-Behind" for *Dark Recesses*, "The Moleskin Cap" for *Ideomancer*, "The Woodwoose" for *Murky Depths*, "Weeping Willows" for *Library of Horror*, "Ravenclaw" for *Fantasy Magazine*, and . . . well, you get the picture. As for Books, my short story collection, *Bridges to the Imagination* is now being considered by Sam's Dot Publishing along with my third novel, *I Gnome, Rising of a Wizard*. Writing is an obsession, a curse, a blessing, a passionate endeavor, a distraction, a gift, and an exercise in humility all rolled up in one bright ball.

CRS Bailey

CRS Bailey was raised in Memphis, TN under a last name both unpronounceable and impossible to spell. The early challenge of name-writing with such a cumbersome surname did not stifle her interest in writing more interesting things. By six, the family knew she had an interest in storytelling. By seventeen, she was a paid, published author, and a journalist for the *Teen Appeal*. Now a journalism major at Indiana University with a year until graduation, Bailey continues to find pleasure in writing science fiction and fantasy short stories, and editing everything she can get her hands on, especially the Internet.

J L Mulvihill

J L Mulvihill is the author of *The Lost Daughter of Easa,* which is the first book of a young adult fantasy series that borders on science fiction with a dash of steampunk. She has been writing poetry, short stories, and song lyrics since she has been able to write and rhyme. J L has written several short stories including "A Real Dragon" and "Magic in The Ozarks", found in *Memories and Dreams* published by The Fine Arts Center of Hot Springs, AR; "Jen's Spicy Crawfish Bisque", found in *It's All about Food with a Mississippi Twist*, published through the Clinton Ink-Slingers; and more recently "Chilled Meat", which is found in the *Dreams of Steam II: Bolts and Brass* anthology by Kerlak Publishing. J L is currently working on her second novel, *Elsindai,* while writing short stories and poetry inspired by her life in the South.

Alexander S. Brown

Alexander S. Brown is a Mississippi author originally beginning his writing career in the horror genre but recently branching out to dark fantasy and steampunk. Previous publications include *Traumatized*, which has received rave reviews and was once banned. He was published in *Dreams of Steam 2* with the contribution of "The Third Eye", the first tale introducing Xavier Hess. Future works include *Syrenthia Falls*. Currently, he is penning his second book in an unnamed horror fantasy series.

Alexander S. Brown would like to thank Herika Raymer and Louise Myers for their great editorial services. Learn more at:
www.traumatizedalexandersbrown.webs.com.

Anne E. Barringer

Anne wrote her first story at age seven after discovering an insatiable love for words and a need to consume most things written. Since then story ideas get penned on unusual surfaces including legal file boxes and her own arms. Besides reviewing books for online websites, she worked as a paralegal/office manager and helped keep the signal going as the 2009 Global Organizer of CSTS. Nonetheless, writing is #1 in her heart.

Born in Louisville, KY, she's lived in many places including Brandon, FL, Topeka, KS (where daughters Beth, Marissa and grand-baby Nina-Bee live) and Memphis, TN. However, the amazing Eureka, CA with its oceans, and redwood-forest-covered mountains is where her heart calls home with Phil (her groom of twenty years) and Awen her wire-hair dachshund muse. If she's not working on her latest short story or young adult novel, you can find her volunteering, reading, a"muse"ing others, cooking and playing with all things photography-like.

Mandi M. Lynch

Mandi M. Lynch started writing stories at the age of six, when she would peck the words with one finger. While the crayon drawings have improved marginally, the spelling has not. Lynch currently runs *Ink Monkey Magazine*, and is editing several anthologies including *Soundtrack Not Included*: The Nashville Writers Meetup 2011 Anthology, and *You Must Read This*, an anthology of second person stories. She also runs several writers groups for the NWMG and the Office of Letters and Light. Lynch can often be found in the corner of wrongness with her writing friends and a herd of stuffed moose, and has most recently been published in *Stories from the ePocalypse* through Pill Hill Press. She lives in Nashville, TN, with three cats, none of whom write due to lack of thumbs.

S. P. Dorning

In the latter months of the year 2010, a writing competition was held in the Blount County, and surrounding areas, of Alabama. The winner of this competition was to have his or her book published through Fifth Estate Publishing, a small company that prints authors only by invitation. Stephen Dorning won that competition with his first book *Stars of the Kanri*, a story that was a strange mixture of faith and science fiction. Since then, Stephen has published a sequel to the story with *Spheres of the Ryk-tar* and is currently working on his third story set in the same world. Stephen was born and raised in the rural area of Blountsville, Alabama, where he lives with his wife, Vicki and their four children. He attends Mount Tabor Baptist Church and currently teaches Sunday School to the church's Young Adult class. All of his works are also available on Kindle and Enook.

Nick Valentino

His steampunk adventure novel, *Thomas Riley (Echelon Press/Quake)*, is the first in a series of alternative history/steampunk books about two Victorian-era weapons designers that are forced into enemy lands to undo an alchemic mishap. The second installment of the series, *Thomas Riley~ The Aurora*, is due out in 2012 (ZOVA Books). Valentino's Weird West story, "Engine 316" is included in the *Dreams of Steam* anthology (Kerlak Publishing), and steampunk horror short, "Bedeviled" in *Dreams of Steam II* (Kerlak Publishing). His story, "Ten Thousand Years" is a Japanese Steampunk story featured in Echelon Press' anthology *Her Majesty's Mysterious Conveyance* and his story, "Double Crossed at Gray Raven Mill" is included in *Steampunk Tales* Issue #8.

Henry Lewis Sanders

He recently had his chapbook of science fiction and horror ku, *Dark Eden*, released by Sam's Dot Publishing in paperback. Please note Henry writes his fiction under his full name Henry Lewis Sanders and his poetry under his middle name Lewis Sanders. Ku is a short poetry form based on the poetic form of haiku. And Henry does so like to descend into the dark, bloody realm of the vampire in his poetry and fiction. Recent poetry has been accepted by *Cover of Darkness*, *Hungur* magazine and his poetry has appeared in *Gore Creatures*. *Blood Journey: A Vampire Novel* by Henry Lewis Sanders and Terrie Leigh Relf is now in paperback at Sam's Dot Publishing. Haiku under his name 'Lewis Sanders' has appeared in *Modern Haiku, Dragonfly, A Quarterly Of Haiku, Parnassus Literary Journal* and *Lynx* magazine. *Lynx* is a journal of *renga* edited and published by Jane Reichhold. *Blood Journey* is now on e-book at www.smashwords.com

Windsong Levitch

Windsong is an Ojibway Native America. She attended college in California. Although retired now, she is a Dr. of Zoology .She has been writing since her early teens. Her first book, *The Lighter Side of Dark,* was published in 2009. It is a collection of Gothic and fantasy poems and short stories. She also has a poem in *Dragons Composed.* Windsong also has many short stories and poems in *Imagyro Magazine.* Born in Manomen, Minnesota on Red Lake Indian Reservation, she has traveled extensively and speaks many languages. Windsong and her husband now live in the Memphis Tennessee area with their many cats on their mini farm. A Polio survivor, she has accomplished a great deal, but if asked what is her greatest accomplishment, she will smile and say "I am a wife, mother and grandmother."

Michael Greenway

Michael Greenway is a hobby Haiku poet since 2005 and a former theme park blogger with *TheRapidsBlog* (2008-2011). He also has enjoyed hobby photography since 2006. His current creative energy is focused on guitar (started in 1994), martial arts (also started in 1994) and cosplay endeavors.

*Discover other fine Kerlak
publications at:*

http://www.kerlakpublishing.com

CPSIA information can be obtained at www.ICGtesting.com
Printed in the USA
LVOW060109180413

329657LV00001B/3/P

9 781937 035105